Ella
Enchanted

GAIL CARSON LEVINE

HARPERCOLLINS*PUBLISHERS*

Ella Enchanted

For information address HarperCollins Children's Books, a division of HarperCollins Publishers, 10 East 53rd Street, New York, NY 10022.

Library of Congress Cataloging-in-Publication Data
Levine, Gail Carson.
Ella enchanted / Gail Carson Levine.
p. cm.
Summary: In this novel based on the story of Cinderella, Ella struggles against the childhood curse that forces her to obey any order given to her.
ISBN 0-06-027510-3. — ISBN 0-06-027511-1 (lib. bdg.)
[1. Fantasy.] I. Title.
PZ7.L578345El 1997 96-30734
[Fic]—dc20 CIP
AC

Typography by Al Cetta
9 10

❖

TO DAVID. MORE TUNES.

Ella Enchanted

CHAPTER ONE

That fool of a fairy Lucinda did not intend to lay a curse on me. She meant to bestow a gift. When I cried inconsolably through my first hour of life, my tears were her inspiration. Shaking her head sympathetically at Mother, the fairy touched my nose. "My gift is obedience. Ella will always be obedient. Now stop crying, child."

I stopped.

Father was away on a trading expedition as usual, but our cook, Mandy, was there. She and Mother were horrified, but no matter how they explained it to Lucinda, they couldn't make her understand the terrible thing she'd done to me. I could picture the argument: Mandy's freckles standing out sharper than usual, her frizzy gray hair in disarray, and her double chin shaking with anger; Mother still and intense, her brown curls damp from labor, the laughter gone from her eyes.

I couldn't imagine Lucinda. I didn't know what she looked like.

She wouldn't undo the curse.

My first awareness of it came on my fifth birthday. I seem to remember that day perfectly, perhaps because Mandy told the tale so often.

"For your birthday," she'd start, "I baked a beautiful cake. Six layers."

Bertha, our head maid, had sewn a special gown for me. "Blue as midnight with a white sash. You were small for your age even then, and you looked like a china doll, with a white ribbon in your black hair and your cheeks red from excitement."

In the middle of the table was a vase filled with flowers that Nathan, our manservant, had picked.

We all sat around the table. (Father was away again.) I was thrilled. I had watched Mandy bake the cake and Bertha sew the gown and Nathan pick the flowers.

Mandy cut the cake. When she handed me my piece, she said without thinking, "Eat."

The first bite was delicious. I finished the slice happily. When it was gone, Mandy cut another. That one was harder. When it was gone, no one gave me more, but I knew I had to keep eating. I moved my fork into the cake itself.

"Ella, what are you doing?" Mother said.

"Little piggy." Mandy laughed. "It's her birthday, Lady. Let her have as much as she wants." She put another slice on my plate.

I felt sick, and frightened. Why couldn't I stop eating?

Swallowing was a struggle. Each bite weighed on my tongue and felt like a sticky mass of glue as I fought to get it down. I started crying while I ate.

Mother realized first. "Stop eating, Ella," she commanded.

I stopped.

Anyone could control me with an order. It had to be a direct command, such as "Put on a shawl," or "You

must go to bed now." A wish or a request had no effect. I was free to ignore "I wish you would put on a shawl," or "Why don't you go to bed now?" But against an order I was powerless.

If someone told me to hop on one foot for a day and a half, I'd have to do it. And hopping on one foot wasn't the worst order I could be given. If you commanded me to cut off my own head, I'd have to do it.

I was in danger at every moment.

As I grew older, I learned to delay my obedience, but each moment cost me dear—in breathlessness, nausea, dizziness, and other complaints. I could never hold out for long. Even a few minutes were a desperate struggle.

I had a fairy godmother, and Mother asked her to take the curse away. But my fairy godmother said Lucinda was the only one who could remove it. However, she also said it might be broken someday without Lucinda's help.

But I didn't know how. I didn't even know who my fairy godmother was.

Instead of making me docile, Lucinda's curse made a rebel of me. Or perhaps I was that way naturally.

Mother rarely insisted I do anything. Father knew nothing of the curse and saw me too infrequently to issue many commands. But Mandy was bossy, giving orders almost as often as she drew breath. Kind orders or for-your-own-good orders. "Bundle up, Ella." Or "Hold this bowl while I beat the eggs, sweet."

I disliked these commands, harmless as they were. I'd hold the bowl, but move my feet so she would have to follow me around the kitchen. She'd call me minx and

try to hem me in with more specific instructions, which I would find new ways to evade. Often, it was a long business to get anything done between us, with Mother laughing and egging each of us on by turn.

We'd end happily—with me finally choosing to do what Mandy wanted, or with Mandy changing her order to a request.

When Mandy would absentmindedly give me an order I knew she didn't mean, I'd say, "Do I have to?" And she'd reconsider.

When I was eight, I had a friend, Pamela, the daughter of one of the servants. One day she and I were in the kitchen, watching Mandy make marchpane. When Mandy sent me to the pantry for more almonds, I returned with only two. She ordered me back with more exact instructions, which I followed exactly, while still managing to frustrate her true wishes.

Later, when Pamela and I retreated to the garden to devour the candy, she asked why I hadn't done what Mandy wanted straight off.

"I hate when she's bossy," I answered.

Pamela said smugly, "I always obey my elders."

"That's because you don't have to."

"I do have to, or Father will slap me."

"It's not the same as for me. I'm under a spell." I enjoyed the importance of the words. Spells were rare. Lucinda was the only fairy rash enough to cast them on people.

"Like Sleeping Beauty?"

"Except I won't have to sleep for a hundred years."

"What's your spell?"

I told her.

"If anybody gives you an order, you have to obey? Including me?"

I nodded.

"Can I try it?"

"No." I hadn't anticipated this. I changed the subject. "I'll race you to the gate."

"All right, but I command you to lose the race."

"Then I don't want to race."

"I command you to race, and I command you to lose."

We raced. I lost.

We picked berries. I had to give Pamela the sweetest, ripest ones. We played princesses and ogres. I had to be the ogre.

An hour after my admission, I punched her. She screamed, and blood poured from her nose.

Our friendship ended that day. Mother found Pamela's mother a new situation far from our town of Frell.

After punishing me for using my fist, Mother issued one of her infrequent commands: never to tell anyone about my curse. But I wouldn't have anyway. I had learned caution.

When I was almost fifteen, Mother and I caught cold. Mandy dosed us with her curing soup, made with carrots, leeks, celery, and hair from a unicorn's tail. It was delicious, but we both hated to see those long yellow-white hairs floating around the vegetables.

Since Father was away from Frell, we drank the soup sitting up in Mother's bed. If he had been home, I wouldn't have been in her room at all. He didn't like me to be anywhere near him, getting underfoot, as he said.

I sipped my soup with the hairs in it because Mandy had said to, even though I grimaced at the soup and at Mandy's retreating back.

"I'll wait for mine to cool," Mother said. Then, after Mandy left, she took the hairs out while she ate and put them back in the empty bowl when she was done.

The next day I was well and Mother was much worse, too sick to drink or eat anything. She said there was a knife in her throat and a battering ram at her head. To make her feel better, I put cool cloths on her forehead and told her stories. They were only old, familiar tales about the fairies that I changed here and there, but sometimes I made Mother laugh. Except the laugh would turn into a cough.

Before Mandy sent me off for the night, Mother kissed me. "Good night. I love you, precious."

They were her last words to me. As I left the room, I heard her last words to Mandy. "I'm not very sick. Don't send for Sir Peter."

Sir Peter was Father.

The next morning, she was awake, but dreaming. With wide-open eyes, she chattered to invisible courtiers and plucked nervously at her silver necklace. To Mandy and me, there in the room with her, she said nothing.

Nathan, the manservant, got the physician, who hurried me away from Mother's side.

Our hallway was empty. I followed it to the spiral staircase and walked down, remembering the times Mother and I had slid down the banister.

We didn't do it when people were around. "We have to be dignified," she would whisper then, stepping down the stairs in an especially stately way. And I would follow, mimicking her and fighting my natural clumsiness, pleased to be part of her game.

But when we were alone, we preferred to slide and yell all the way down. And run back up for another ride, and a third, and a fourth.

When I got to the bottom of the stairs, I pulled our heavy front door open and slipped out into bright sunshine.

It was a long walk to the old castle, but I wanted to make a wish, and I wanted to make it in the place where it would have the best chance of being granted.

The castle had been abandoned when King Jerrold was a boy, although it was reopened on special occasions, for private balls, weddings, and the like. Even so, Bertha said it was haunted, and Nathan said it was infested with mice. Its gardens were overgrown, but Bertha swore the candle trees had power.

I went straight to the candle grove. The candles were small trees that had been pruned and tied to wires to make them grow in the shape of candelabra.

For wishes you need trading material. I closed my eyes and thought.

"If Mother gets well quick, I'll be good, not just obedient. I'll try harder not to be clumsy and I won't tease Mandy so much."

I didn't bargain for Mother's life, because I didn't believe she was in danger of dying.

CHAPTER TWO

Leaving behind a grieving husband and child. We must comfort them." High Chancellor Thomas wound down after droning on for almost an hour. Some of his speech had been about Mother. At least, the words "Lady Eleanor" were spoken often, but the person they described—dutiful parent, loyal citizen, steadfast spouse—sounded more like the high chancellor than like my mother. Part of the speech had been about dying, but more was about giving allegiance to Kyrria and its rulers, King Jerrold, Prince Charmont, and the entire royal family.

Father reached for my hand. His palm was moist and hot as a hydra's swamp. I wished I had been allowed to stand with Mandy and the other servants.

I pulled out of his grasp and moved a step away. He closed the distance between us and took my hand again.

Mother's casket was made of gleaming mahogany carved with designs of fairies and elves. If only the fairies could leap out of the wood and cast a spell to bring her back to life. And another one to send Father away. Or maybe my fairy godmother would do it, if I knew where to find her.

When the high chancellor finished, it was my task to close the casket so Mother could be lowered into her grave. Father put his hands on my shoulders and pushed me forward.

Mother's mouth was stern, the opposite of its look in life. And her face was empty, which was awful. But worse was the creak as the coffin lid went down and the dry click when it closed. And the thought of Mother packed away in a box.

The tears I had swallowed all day erupted. I stood there before the whole court, crying in an infant's endless wail, unable to stop myself.

Father pressed my face into his chest. Perhaps he appeared to be comforting me, but he was only trying to muffle my noise, which couldn't be muffled. He let me go. In a sharp whisper, he said, "Get away from here. Come back when you can be quiet."

For once I was glad to obey. I ran. My heavy black gown tripped me, and I fell. Before anyone could help me, I was off again, my knee and hand stinging.

The biggest tree in the graveyard was a weeping willow—a crying tree. I plunged through its leaves and threw myself down, sobbing.

Everyone called it losing Mother, but she wasn't lost. She was gone, and no matter where I went—another town, another country, Fairyland, or Gnome Caverns—I wouldn't find her.

We'd never talk again, or laugh together. Or swim in the River Lucarno. Or slide down the banister or play tricks on Bertha. Or a million things.

I cried myself out and sat up. My gown had changed in front from black silk to brown dirt. As Mandy would have said, I was a spectacle.

How much time had gone by? I had to go back.

Father had told me to, and the curse was tugging at me to obey.

Outside the privacy of my tree, Prince Charmont stood, reading a tombstone. I had never been so near him before. Had he heard me cry?

Although the prince was only two years older than I, he was much taller, and he stood just like his father, feet apart, hands behind his back, as though the whole country were passing by on review. He looked like his father too, although the sharp angles of King Jerrold's face were softened in his son. They each had tawny curls and swarthy skin. I had never been near enough to the king to know whether he also had a sprinkling of freckles across his nose, surprising on such a dark face.

"Cousin of mine," the prince said, gesturing at the tombstone. "Never liked him. I liked your mother." He started walking back toward her tomb.

Did he expect me to come with him? Was I supposed to maintain a suitable distance from his royal self?

With enough room for a carriage to pass between us, I walked at his side. He moved closer. I saw he had been crying too, although he had stayed upright and clean.

"You can call me Char," he told me suddenly. "Everyone else does."

I could? We walked in silence.

"My father calls me Char too," he added.

The king!

"Thank you," I said.

"Thank you, Char," he corrected. Then, "Your mother used to make me laugh. Once, at a banquet, Chancellor Thomas was making a speech. While he talked, your mother moved her napkin around. I saw it before your father crumpled it up. She had arranged the edge in the shape of the chancellor's profile, with the mouth open and the chin stuck out. It would have looked exactly like him if he were the color of a blue napkin. I had to leave without dinner so I could go outside and laugh."

We were halfway back. It was starting to rain. I could make out one figure, small in the distance, standing by Mother's grave. Father.

"Where did everyone go?" I asked Char.

"They all left before I came to find you," he said. "Did you want them to wait?" He sounded worried, as if, perhaps, he should have made them stay.

"No, I didn't want any of them to wait," I answered, meaning Father could have gone too.

"I know all about you," Char announced after we'd taken a few more steps.

"You do? How could you?"

"Your cook and our cook meet at the market. She talks about you." He looked sideways at me. "Do you know much about me?"

"No." Mandy had never said anything. "What do you know?"

"I know you can imitate people just as Lady Eleanor could. Once you imitated your manservant to his face, and he wasn't sure whether he was the servant or you were. You make up your own fairy tales and you drop things and trip over things. I know you once broke a whole set of dishes."

"I slipped on ice!"

"Ice chips you spilled before you slipped on them." He laughed. It wasn't a ridiculing laugh; it was a happy laugh at a good joke.

"An accident," I protested. But I smiled too, tremblingly, after so much crying.

We reached Father, who bowed. "Thank you, Highness, for accompanying my daughter."

Char returned the bow.

"Come, Eleanor," Father said.

Eleanor. No one had ever called me that before, even though it was my real name. Eleanor had always been Mother, and always would be.

"Ella. I'm Ella," I said.

"Ella then. Come, Ella." He bowed to Prince Charmont and climbed into the carriage.

I had to go. Char handed me in. I didn't know whether to give him my hand or to let him push up on my elbow. He wound up with the middle of my arm and I had to grasp the side of the carriage with the other hand for balance. When he closed the door, I caught my skirt, and there was a loud ripping sound. Father winced. I saw Char through the window, laughing again. I turned the skirt and found a gash about six inches above the hem. Bertha would never be able to make it smooth.

I arranged myself as far from Father as possible. He was staring out the window.

"A fine affair. All of Frell came, everyone who counts anyway," he said, as though Mother's funeral had been a tournament or a ball.

"It wasn't fine. It was awful," I said. How could Mother's funeral be fine?

"The prince was friendly to you."

"He liked Mother."

"Your mother was beautiful." His voice was regretful. "I'm sorry she's dead."

Nathan flicked his whip, and the carriage began to move.

CHAPTER THREE

When we reached the manor, Father ordered me to change into something clean and to hurry down to greet the guests who were arriving to pay their respects.

My room was peaceful. Everything was just as it had been before Mother died. The birds embroidered into the coverlet on my bed were safe in their world of cross-stitched leaves. My diary was on the dresser. The friends of my childhood—Flora, the rag doll, and Rosamunde, the wooden doll in the gown with seven flounces—nestled in their basket.

I sat on the bed, fighting my need to obey Father's order to change and go back downstairs. Although I wanted to draw comfort from my room, from my bed, from the light breeze coming through my window, I kept thinking instead of Father and getting dressed.

Once I had overheard Bertha tell Mandy that he was only a person on the outside and that his insides were ashes mixed with coins and a brain.

But Mandy had disagreed. "He's human through and through. No other creature would be as selfish as he is, not fairies or gnomes or elves or giants."

For a full three minutes I delayed getting dressed. It was a terrible game I played, trying to break my curse, seeing how long I could last against the need to do what I had been told. There was a buzzing in my ears, and the floor seemed to tilt so far that I feared I would slide off the bed. I hugged my pillow until my arms hurt—as if the pillow were an anchor against following orders.

In a second I was going to fly apart into a thousand pieces. I stood and walked to my wardrobe. Immediately I felt perfectly fine.

Although I suspected Father wanted me to wear another mourning gown, I put on the frock Mother liked best. She said the spicy green brought out my eyes. I thought I looked like a grasshopper in it—a skinny, spiky grasshopper with a human head and straight hair. But at least the gown wasn't black. She hated black clothing.

The great hall was full of people in black. Father came to me instantly. "Here's my lass, young Eleanor," he said loudly. He led me in, whispering, "You look like a weed in that gown. You're supposed to be in mourning. They'll think you have no respect for your—"

I was engulfed from behind by two chubby arms encased in rustling black satin.

"My poor child, we feel for you." The voice was syrupy. "And Sir Peter, it's dreadful to see you on such a tragic occasion." An extra tight squeeze and I was released.

The speaker was a tall, plump lady with long and wavy honey-colored tresses. Her face was a pasty white with twin spots of rouge on the cheeks. With her were two smaller versions of herself, but without the rouge. The younger one also lacked her mother's abundant hair; instead she had thin curls stuck tight to her scalp as though glued there.

"This is Dame Olga," Father said, touching the tall lady's arm.

I curtsied and knocked into the younger girl. "Beg pardon," I said.

She didn't answer, didn't move, only watched me.

Father continued. "Are these your lovely daughters?"

"They are my treasures. This is Hattie, and this is Olive. They are off to finishing school in a few days."

Hattie was older than I, by about two years. "Delighted to make your acquaintance," she said, smiling and showing large front teeth. She held her hand out to me as though she expected me to kiss it or bow over it.

I stared, uncertain what to do. She lowered her arm, but continued to smile.

Olive was the one I'd bumped. "I'm glad to meet you," she said, her voice too loud. She was about my age. The furrows of a frown were permanently etched between her eyes.

"Comfort Eleanor in her grief," Dame Olga told her daughters. "I want to talk with Sir Peter." She took Father's arm, and they left us.

"Our hearts weep for you," Hattie began. "When you bellowed at the funeral, I thought what a poor thing you are."

"Green isn't a mourning color," Olive said.

Hattie surveyed the room. "This is a fine hall, almost as fine as the palace, where I'm going to live someday. Our mother, Dame Olga, says your father is very rich. She says he can make money out of anything."

"Out of a toenail," Olive suggested.

"Our mother, Dame Olga, says your father was poor when he married your mother. Our mother says Lady Eleanor was rich when they got married, but your father made her richer."

"We're rich too," Olive said. "We're lucky to be rich."

"Would you show us the rest of the manor?" Hattie asked.

We went upstairs and Hattie had to look everywhere. She opened the wardrobe in Mother's room and, before I could stop her, ran her hands over Mother's gowns. When we got back to the hall, she announced, "Forty-two windows and a fireplace in every room. The windows must have cost a trunkful of gold KJs."

"Do you want to know about our manor?" Olive asked.

I didn't care if they lived in a hollow log.

"You'll have to visit us and see for yourself," Hattie said in response to my silence.

We stood near the side table, which was loaded with mountains of food, from a whole roast hart with ivy threaded through its antlers to butter cookies as small and lacy as snowflakes. I wondered how Mandy had had time to cook it all.

"Would you like something to eat?"

"Ye—" Olive began, but her sister interrupted firmly.

"Oh, no. No thank you. We never eat at parties. The excitement quite takes away our appetites."

"My appetite—" Olive tried again.

"Our appetites are small. Mother worries. But it looks delicious." Hattie edged toward the food. "Quail eggs are such a delicacy. Ten brass KJs apiece. Olive, there are fifty at least."

More quail eggs than windows.

"I like gooseberry tarts," Olive said.

"We mustn't," Hattie said. "Well, maybe a little."

A giant couldn't eat half a leg of deer plus a huge mound of wild rice and eight of the fifty quail eggs and go back for dessert. But Hattie could.

Olive ate even more. Gooseberry tarts and currant bread and cream trifle and plum pudding and chocolate bonbons and spice cake—all dribbled over with butter rum sauce and apricot sauce and peppermint sauce.

They brought their plates close to their faces so their forks had the shortest possible distance to travel. Olive ate steadily, but Hattie put her fork down every so often to pat her mouth daintily with her napkin. Then she'd tuck in again, as avidly as ever.

It was disgusting to watch. I looked down at a throw rug that used to lie under Mother's chair. Today it had been moved near the food. I had never concentrated on it before.

A hound and hunters chased a boar toward a fringe of scarlet wool. As I stared, I saw movement. Wind stirred the grass by the boar's feet. I blinked and the movement stopped. I stared again and it started again.

The dog had just bayed. I felt his throat relax. One of the hunters limped, and I felt a cramp in his calf. The boar gasped for breath and ran on fear and rage.

"What are you looking at?" Olive asked. She had finished eating.

I started. I felt as if I'd been in the rug. "Nothing. Just the carpet." I glanced at the rug again. An ordinary carpet with an ordinary design.

"Your eyes were popping out."

"They looked like an ogre's eyes," Hattie said. "Buggy. But there, you look more normal now."

She never looked normal. She looked like a rabbit. A fat one, the kind Mandy liked to slaughter for stew. And Olive's face was as blank as a peeled potato.

"I don't suppose your eyes ever pop out," I said.

"I don't think so." Hattie smiled complacently.

"They're too small to pop."

The smile remained, but now it seemed pasted on. "I forgive you, child. We in the peerage are forgiving. Your poor mother used to be known for her ill breeding too."

Mother used to be known. The past tense froze my tongue.

"Girls!" Dame Olga bore down on us. "We must be going." She hugged me, and my nose filled with the stink of spoiled milk.

They left. Father was outside at the iron gate, saying good-bye to the rest of the guests. I went to Mandy in the kitchen.

She was piling up dirty dishes. "Seems like those people didn't eat for a week."

I put on an apron and pumped water into the sink. "They never tasted your food before."

Mandy's cooking was better than anybody else's. Mother and I used to try her recipes sometimes. We'd follow the instructions exactly and the dish would be delicious, but never as wonderful as when Mandy cooked it.

Somehow, it reminded me of the rug. "The carpet in the hall with the hunters and the boar, you know the one? Something funny happened to me when I looked at it before."

"Oh, that silly thing. You shouldn't pay attention to that old rug." She turned to stir a pot of soup.

"What do you mean?"

"It's just a fairy joke."

A fairy rug! "How do you know?"

"It belonged to Lady." Mandy always called Mother "Lady."

That wasn't an answer. "Did my fairy godmother give it to her?"

"A long time ago."

"Did Mother ever tell you who my fairy godmother is?"

"No, she didn't. Where's your father?"

"He's outside, saying good-bye. Do you know anyway? Even though she never told you?"

"Know what?"

"Who my fairy godmother is."

"If she'd wanted you to know, your mother would have told you."

"She was going to. She promised. Please tell, Mandy."

"I am."

"You are *not* telling. Who is it?"

"Me. Your fairy godmother is me. Here, taste the carrot soup. It's for dinner. How is it?"

CHAPTER FOUR

My mouth opened automatically. The spoon descended and a hot—but not burning—swallow poured in. Mandy had gotten the carrots at their sweetest, carrotiest best. Weaving in and out of the carrots were other flavors: lemon, turtle broth, and a spice I couldn't name. The best carrot soup in the world, magical soup that nobody but Mandy could make.

The rug. The soup. This was fairy soup. Mandy was a fairy!

But if Mandy was a fairy, why was Mother dead?

"You're not a fairy."

"Why not?"

"If you were, you would have saved her."

"Oh, sweetie, I would have if I could. If she'd left the hair in my curing soup, she'd be well today."

"You knew? Why did you let her?"

"I didn't know till she was too sick. We can't stop dying."

I collapsed on the stool next to the stove, sobbing so hard I couldn't catch my breath. Then Mandy's arms were around me, and I was crying into the ruffles along the neck of her apron, where I had cried so many times before for smaller reasons.

A drop landed on my finger. Mandy was crying too.

Her face was red and blotchy.

"I was her fairy godmother too," Mandy said. "And your grandmother's." She blew her nose.

I pushed out of Mandy's arms for a new look at her. She couldn't be a fairy. Fairies were thin and young and beautiful. Mandy was as tall as a fairy was supposed to be, but who ever heard of a fairy with frizzy gray hair and two chins?

"Show me," I demanded.

"Show you what?"

"That you're a fairy. Disappear or something."

"I don't have to show you anything. And—with the exception of Lucinda—fairies never disappear when other creatures are present."

"Can you?"

"We can, but we don't. Lucinda is the only one who's rude enough and stupid enough."

"Why is it stupid?"

"Because it lets people know you're a fairy." She started to wash the dishes. "Help me."

"Do Nathan and Bertha know?" I carried plates to the sink.

"Know what?"

"You're a fairy."

"Oh, that again. No one knows but you. And you'd better keep it a secret." Mandy looked her fiercest.

"Why?"

She just scowled.

"I will. I promise. But why?"

"I'll tell you. People only like the idea of fairies. When they bump up against a particular, real-as-corn fairy, there's always trouble." She rinsed a platter. "You dry."

"Why?"

"Because the dishes are wet, that's why." She saw my surprised face. "Oh, why is there trouble? Two reasons, mostly. People know we can do magic, so they want us to solve their problems for them. When we don't, they get mad. The other reason is we're immortal. That gets them mad too. Lady wouldn't speak to me for a week when her father died."

"Why doesn't Lucinda care if people know she's a fairy?"

"She likes them to know, the fool. She wants them to thank her when she gives them one of her awful gifts."

"Are they always awful?"

"Always. They are always awful, but some people are delighted to have a present from a fairy, even if it makes them miserable."

"Why did Mother know you're a fairy? Why do I know?"

"All the Eleanor line are Friends of the Fairies. You have fairy blood in you."

Fairy blood! "Can I do magic? Shall I live forever? Would Mother have if she hadn't gotten sick? Are there many Friends of the Fairies?"

"Very few. You're the only one left in Kyrria. And no, love, you can't do magic or live forever. It's just a drop of fairy blood. But there's one way it has already started to show. Your feet haven't grown for a few years, I'll warrant."

"None of me has grown for a few years."

"The rest of you will soon enough, but you'll have fairy feet, like your mother did." Mandy lifted the hems of her skirt and five petticoats to reveal feet that were no longer than mine. "We're too tall for our feet. It's the only thing we can't change by magic. Our men stuff their shoes so no one can tell, and we ladies hide them under our skirts."

I stuck a foot out of my gown. Tiny feet were fashionable, but would they make me even clumsier as I grew taller? Would I be able to keep my balance?

"Could you make my feet grow if you wanted to? Or . . . " I searched for another miracle. Rain pelted the window. "Or could you stop the rain?"

Mandy nodded.

"Do it. Please do it."

"Why would I want to?"

"For me. I want to see magic. Big magic."

"We don't do big magic. Lucinda's the only one. It's too dangerous."

"What's dangerous about ending a storm?"

"Maybe nothing, maybe something. Use your imagination."

"Clear skies would be good. People could go outside."

"Use your imagination," Mandy repeated.

I thought. "The grass needs rain. The crops need rain."

"More," Mandy said.

"Maybe a bandit was going to rob someone, and he isn't doing it because of the weather."

"That's right. Or maybe I'd start a drought, and then I'd have to fix that because I started it. And then maybe the rain I sent would knock down a branch and smash in the roof of a house, and I'd have to fix that too."

"That wouldn't be your fault. The owners should have built a stronger roof."

"Maybe, maybe not. Or maybe I'd cause a flood and people would be killed. That's the problem with big magic. I only do little magic. Good cooking, my curing soup, my Tonic."

"When Lucinda cast the spell on me, was that big magic?"

"Of course it was. The numskull!" Mandy scoured a pot so hard that it clattered and banged against the copper sink.

"Tell me how to break the spell. Please, Mandy."

"I don't know how. I only know it can be done."

"If I told Lucinda how terrible it is, would she lift the spell, do you think?"

"I doubt it, but maybe. Then again, she might take away one spell and give you another even worse. The trouble with Lucinda is, ideas pop into her head and come out as spells."

"What does she look like?"

"Not like the rest of us. But you'd better hope you never lay eyes on her."

"Where does she live?" I asked. If I could find her, maybe I could persuade her to lift my curse. After all, Mandy could be wrong.

"We're not on speaking terms. I don't keep track of the whereabouts of Lucinda the Idiot. Watch that bowl!"

The order came too late. I got the broom. "Are all Friends clumsy?"

"No, sweet. Fairy blood does not make you clumsy. That's human. You don't see me dropping plates, do you?"

I started to sweep, but it wasn't necessary. The pieces of pottery gathered themselves together and flew into the trash bin. I couldn't believe it.

"That's about all I do, honey. Small magic that can't hurt anybody. Handy sometimes, though. No sharp bits left on the floor."

I stared into the bin. The shards lay there. "Why didn't you turn it back into a bowl?"

"The magic's too big. Doesn't seem like it, but it is. Could hurt someone. You never know."

"You mean fairies can't see the future? If you could, you'd know, wouldn't you?"

"We can't see the future any more than you can. Only gnomes can, a few of them anyway."

A bell tinkled somewhere in the house. Father calling one of the servants. Mother never used the bell.

"Were you my great-grandmother's fairy godmother too?" A thousand questions flooded in. "How long have you been our fairy godmother?" How old was Mandy, really?

Bertha came in. "Sir Peter wants you in the study, miss."

"What does he want?" I asked.

"He didn't say." She twisted one of her braids anxiously.

Bertha was scared of everything. What was there to be afraid of? My father wanted to talk to me. It was only to be expected.

I finished drying a plate, dried another, then a third.

"Best not tarry, little mistress," Bertha said.

I reached for a fourth dish.

"You'd better go," Mandy said. "And he won't want to see that apron."

Mandy was frightened too! I took off the apron and left.

I stopped just within the doorway of the study. Father sat in Mother's chair, examining something in his lap.

"Ah, there you are." He looked up. "Come closer, Ella."

I glared at him, resenting the order. Then I took one step forward. It was the game I played with Mandy, obedience and defiance.

"I asked you to come closer, Eleanor."

"I came closer."

"Not near enough. I won't bite you. I only want to get to know you a bit." He walked to me and led me to a chair facing him.

"Have you ever seen anything as splendid as this?" He passed me the object he'd had in his lap. "You can hold it. It's heavy for its size. Here."

I decided to drop it since he liked it so much. But I glanced at it first, and then I couldn't.

I held a porcelain castle no bigger than my two fists, with six wee towers, each ending in a miniature candle holder. And oh! Strung between a window in each of two towers was a gossamer thread of china from which hung—laundry! A man's hose, a robe, a baby's pinafore, all thin as a spider's web. And, painted in a window downstairs, a smiling maiden waved a silken scarf. It seemed to be silk, anyway.

Father took it from me. "Close your eyes."

I heard him pull the heavy drapes shut. I watched through slitted eyes. I didn't trust him.

He placed the castle on the mantel, put in candles, and lit them.

"Open your eyes."

I ran to look closer. The castle was a sparkling wonderland. The flames drew pearly tints out of the white walls, and the windows glowed yellow-gold, suggesting cheerful fires within.

"Ohhh!" I said.

Father opened the drapes and blew out the candles. "Lovely, isn't it?"

I nodded. "Where did you get it?"

"From the elves. An elf made it. They're marvelous potters. One of Agulen's students made this. I've always wanted an Agulen, but I haven't got any yet."

"Where will you put it?"

"Where do you want me to put it, Ella?"

"In a window."

"Not in your room?"

"In any room, but in a window." So it could wink out at everyone, inside and on the street.

Father stared at me for a long moment. "I shall tell its buyer to place it in a window."

"You're going to sell it!"

"I'm a merchant, Ella. I sell things." For a minute he spoke to himself. "And perhaps I can pass this one off as a genuine Agulen. Who could tell?" He came back to me. "Now you know who I am: Sir Peter, the merchant. But who are you?"

"A daughter who used to have a mother."

He waved that aside. "But who is Ella?"

"A lass who doesn't wish to be interrogated."

He was pleased. "You have courage, to speak to me so." He looked me over. "That's my chin." He touched it, and I drew back. "Strong. Determined. That's my nose. I hope you don't mind that the nostrils flare. My eyes, except yours are green. Most of your face belongs to me. I wonder how it will be on a woman when you grow up."

Why did he think it was fine to talk about me as though I were a portrait instead of a maiden?

"What shall I do with you?" he asked himself.

"Why must you do something with me?"

"I can't leave you to grow up a cook's helper. You must be educated." He changed the subject. "What did you think of Dame Olga's daughters?"

"They were not comforting," I said.

Father laughed, really laughed, head back, shoulders heaving.

What was so funny? I disliked being laughed at. It made me want to say something nice about the loathsome Hattie and Olive. "They meant well, I suppose."

Father wiped tears from his eyes. "They didn't mean well. The older one is an unpleasant conniver like her mother and the younger one is a simpleton. It never entered their heads to mean well." His voice became thoughtful. "Dame Olga is titled and rich."

What did that have to do with anything?

"Perhaps I should send you to finishing school with her daughters. You might learn how to walk like the slip of a thing you are and not like a small elephant."

Finishing school! I'd have to leave Mandy. And they'd tell me what to do all the time and I'd have to do it, whatever it was. They'd try to rid me of my clumsiness, but they wouldn't be able to. So they'd punish me, and I'd punish them back, and they'd punish me more.

"Why can't I just stay here?"

"I suppose you could be taught by a governess. If I could find someone . . ."

"I would much rather have a governess, Father. I would study very hard if I had a governess."

"But not otherwise?" His eyebrows rose, but I could tell he was amused. He stood and went to the desk where Mother used to work out our household accounts. "You may go now. I have work to do."

I left. On my way out, I said, "Perhaps small elephants cannot be admitted to finishing school. Perhaps small elephants cannot be finished. Perhaps they . . ." I stopped. He was laughing again.

CHAPTER FIVE

The next night I had to dine with Father. I had trouble sitting down at the table because Bertha had made me wear a fashionable gown, and my petticoat was voluminous.

On Father's plate and mine was sparrowgrass covered with a tarragon-mustard sauce. In front of his plate was a many-faceted crystal goblet.

When I finally managed to settle in my chair, Father signaled to Nathan to pour wine into the goblet. "See how it catches the light, Eleanor." He raised it. "It makes the wine sparkle like a garnet."

"It's pretty."

"Is that all? Just pretty?"

"It's very pretty, I suppose." I refused to love it. He was going to sell it too.

"You may appreciate it more if you drink from it. Have you ever tasted wine?"

Mandy never let me. I reached for the goblet and trailed my balloon sleeves through the sparrowgrass sauce.

But the goblet was too far away. I had to stand. I stood on my skirts and lost my balance, pitching forward. To stop my fall, I brought my arm crashing down on the table and knocked into Father's elbow.

He dropped the goblet. It fell and broke neatly into two pieces, stem severed from body. A red stain spread across the tablecloth, and Father's doublet was dotted with wine.

I steeled myself for his rage, but he surprised me.

"That was stupid of me," he said, dabbing at his clothes with a napkin. "When you came in, I saw you couldn't manage yourself."

Nathan and a serving maid whisked away the tablecloth and broken glass.

"I apologize," I said.

"That won't put the crystal back together, will it?" he snapped, then collected himself. "Your apology is accepted. We will both change our clothes and begin our meal."

I returned in a quarter hour, in an everyday gown.

"It is my fault," Father said, cutting into a sparrowgrass spear. "I've let you grow up an oaf."

"I'm not an oaf!"

Mandy wasn't one to mince words, and she'd never called me that. Clumsy, bumbling, gawky—but never an oaf. Blunderer, lumpkin, fumble-foot—but never an oaf.

"But you're young enough to learn," Father went on. "Someday I may want to take you into civilized company."

"I don't like civilized company."

"I may need civilized company to like you. I've made up my mind. It's off to finishing school with you."

I couldn't go. I wouldn't!

"You said I could have a governess. Wouldn't that be less expensive than sending me away?"

A serving maid whisked away my uneaten sparrowgrass and replaced it with scallops and tomato aspic.

"How kind of you to worry. A governess would be much more expensive. And I haven't the time to interview governesses. In two days, you shall go to finishing school with Dame Olga's daughters."

"I won't."

He continued as though I hadn't spoken. "I'll write a letter to the headmistress, which I shall entrust to you, along with a purse filled with enough KJs to stop her protests against a last-minute pupil."

"I won't go."

"You shall do as I say, Eleanor."

"I won't go."

"Ella . . ." He bit into a scallop and spoke while he chewed. "Your father is not a good man, as the servants have already warned you, unless I miss my guess."

I didn't deny it.

"They may have said I'm selfish, and I am. They may have said I'm impatient, and I am. They may have said I always have my way. And I do."

"I do too," I lied.

He grinned at me admiringly. "My daughter is the bravest wench in Kyrria." The smile vanished, and his mouth tightened into a hard, thin line. "But she shall go to finishing school if I have to take her there myself. And it will not be a pleasant trip if I have to lose time from my trading because of you. Do you understand, Ella?"

Angry, Father reminded me of a carnival toy, a leather fist attached to a coiled spring used in puppet shows. When the spring was released, the fist shot out at a hapless puppet. With Father, it wasn't the fist that frightened me; it was the spring, because the spring determined the force of the blow. The anger in his eyes was so tightly coiled that I didn't know what would happen if his spring were tripped.

I hated being frightened, but I was. "I'll go to finishing school." I couldn't help adding, "But I shall loathe it."

His grin was back. "You are free to loathe or to love, so long as you go."

It was a taste of obedience without an order, and I didn't like it any better than the Lucinda-induced kind. I left the dining room, and he didn't stop me.

It was early evening. In spite of the hour, I went up to my room and donned my nightgown. Then I moved my dolls, Flora and Rosamunde, into bed and climbed in. They had stopped sleeping with me years before, but tonight I needed special comfort.

I gathered them on my stomach and waited for sleep. But sleep was busy elsewhere.

Tears started. I pushed Flora against my face.

"Sweetie . . ." The door opened. It was Mandy with Tonic and a box.

I felt bad enough. "No Tonic, Mandy. I'm fine. Truly."

"Oh, lovey." She put down the Tonic and the box and held me, stroking my forehead.

"I don't want to go," I said into her shoulder.

"I know, honey," she said. She held me for a long while, until I was almost asleep. Then she shifted her weight. "Tonic time."

"I'll skip tonight."

"No you won't. Not tonight, especially. I won't have you getting sick when you need your strength." A spoon came out of her apron. "Take it. Three spoons."

I braced myself. Tonic tasted nutty and good, but it

felt slimy, like swallowing a frog. Each spoonful oozed along my throat. I continued to gulp after it was down, to rid myself of the sensation.

But it made me feel better—a little better. Ready to talk anyway. I settled myself back in Mandy's lap.

"Why did Mother marry him?" This question had troubled me since I was old enough to think about it.

"Until she was his wife, Sir Peter was very sweet to Lady. I didn't trust him, but she wouldn't listen to me. Her family didn't approve because he was poor, which made Lady want him even more, she was that kind-hearted." Mandy's hand stopped its comforting journey up and down my forehead. "Ella, pet, try to keep him from learning about the spell on you."

"Why? What would he do?"

"He likes to have his way too much. He'd use you."

"Mother ordered me not to tell about the curse. But I wouldn't anyway."

"That's right." Her hand went back to work on my forehead. I closed my eyes.

"What will it be like, do you think?"

"At school? Some of the lasses will be lovely. Sit up, sweet. Don't you want your presents?"

I had forgotten about the box. But there had been only one. "Presents?"

"One at a time." Mandy handed me the box I'd seen. "For you, wherever you go your whole life."

Inside the box was a book of fairy tales. I had never seen such beautiful illustrations. They were almost alive. I turned the pages, marveling.

"When you look at it, you can remember me and take comfort."

"I'll save it until I leave, so the stories will be new."

Mandy chuckled. "You won't finish it so fast. It grows on you." She fished in the pocket of her apron and fetched out a tissue-paper packet. "From Lady. She would have wanted you to have it."

It was Mother's necklace. Threads of silver ended almost at my waist in a woven pattern of silver studded with tiny pearls.

"You'll grow into it, sweet, and look as lovely wearing it as your mother did."

"I'll wear it always."

"You'd be wise to keep it under your gown when you go out. It's that valuable. Gnomes made it."

The bell tinkled downstairs. "That father of yours is ringing."

I hugged Mandy and clung to her.

She disentangled herself from my arms. "Let me go, love." Planting a kiss on my cheek, she left.

I settled back into bed, and this time sleep claimed me.

CHAPTER SIX

The next morning, I woke with my fingers curled around Mother's necklace. The clock in King Jerrold's palace was just striking six. Perfect. I wanted to rise early and spend the day saying good-bye to the places I loved best.

I put my gown over the necklace and crept down to the pantry, where I found a tray of freshly baked scones. They were hot, so I tossed two in the air and caught them in my skirt, pulling it out to make a basket. Then, looking down at my breakfast, I ran to the front of the house and right into Father.

He was in the entranceway, waiting for Nathan to bring the carriage around.

"I don't have time for you now, Eleanor. Run off and bang into somebody else. And tell Mandy I'll be back with the bailiff. We'll need lunch."

As instructed, I ran off. Aside from its dangerous aspects, the curse often made a fool of me and was partly the reason I seemed so clumsy. Now I had to bang into someone.

Bertha was carrying wet laundry. When I bumped into her, she dropped her basket. My gowns and stockings and undergarments tumbled onto the tiles. I helped her pick them up, but she was going to have to wash everything over again.

"Little mistress, it's hard enough getting your things ready so quick without having to do it twice," she scolded.

After I apologized, and after I delivered Father's message to Mandy, and after she made me sit down and eat breakfast on a plate, I started for the royal menagerie just outside the walls of the king's palace.

My favorite exhibits were the talking birds and the exotic animals. Except for the hydra in her swamp and the baby dragon, the exotics—the unicorn, the herd of centaurs, and the gryphon family—lived on an island meadow surrounded by an extension of the castle moat.

The dragon was kept in an iron cage. He was beautiful in his tiny ferocity and seemed happiest when flaming, his ruby eyes gleaming evilly.

I bought a morsel of yellow cheese from the stand next to the cage and toasted it in the fire, which was a tricky business, getting close enough for cooking but not so close that the dragon got the treat.

I wondered what King Jerrold planned to do with him when he grew up. I wondered also whether I would be home to learn his fate.

Beyond the dragon, a centaur stood near the moat, gazing at me. Did centaurs like cheese? I walked toward him quietly, hoping he wouldn't gallop off.

"Here," a voice said.

I turned. It was Prince Charmont, offering me an apple.

"Thank you."

Holding out my hand, I edged closer to the moat. The centaur's nostrils flared and he trotted toward me. I tossed the apple. Two other centaurs galloped over, but mine caught the treat and started eating, crunching loudly.

"I always expect them to thank me or to say, 'How dare you stare?' " I said.

"They're not smart enough to talk. See how blank their eyes are." He pointed, teaching me.

I knew all that, but perhaps it was a princely duty to explain matters to one's subjects.

"If they had words," I said, "they wouldn't be able to think of anything to say."

A surprised silence followed. Then Char laughed. "That's funny! You're funny. As the Lady Eleanor was." He looked stricken. "I'm sorry. I didn't mean to remind you."

"I think of her often," I said. Most of the time.

We walked along the edge of the moat.

"Would you like an apple too?" He held out another one.

I wanted to make him laugh again. I pawed the ground with my right foot and tossed my head as though I had a mane. Opening my eyes as wide as they'd go, I stared stupidly at Char and took the apple.

He did laugh. Then he made an announcement. "I like you. I'm quite taken with you." He took a third apple for himself out of the pocket of his cape.

I liked him too. He wasn't haughty or disdainful, or stuffy, as High Chancellor Thomas was.

All the Kyrrians bowed when we passed, and the visiting elves and gnomes did too. I didn't know how to respond, but Char raised his arm each time, bent at the elbow in the customary royal salute. It was habit, natural to him as teaching. I decided on a deep nod. Curtsies often tipped me over.

We came to the parrot cages, my other favorite place. The birds spoke all the languages of the earth: human foreign tongues and the exotic tongues of Gnomic, Elfian, Ogrese, and Abdegi (the language of the giants). I loved to imitate them, even though I didn't know what they were saying.

Simon, their keeper, was my friend. When he saw Char, he bowed low. Then he returned to feeding an orange bird.

"This one's new," he said. "Speaks Gnomic and doesn't shut up."

",fwthchor evtoogh brzzay eerth ymmadboech evtoogh brzzaY" the parrot said.

",fwthchor evtoogh brzzay eerth ymmadboech evtoogh brzzaY" I repeated.

"You speak Gnomic!" Char said.

"I like to make the sounds. I only know what a few words mean."

"She does it just right, doesn't she, your Highness?"

"Fawithkor evtuk brizzay . . ." Char gave up. "It sounded better when you did it."

",achoed dh eejh aphchuZ uochludwaacH" the parrot squawked.

"Do you know what he said?" I asked Simon, who was able to translate occasionally.

Simon shook his head. "Do you know, sir?"

"No. It sounds like gargling."

Other visitors claimed Simon's attention. "Excuse me," he said.

Char watched while I said farewell to each bird.

".iqkwo pwach brzzay ufedjeE" That was Gnomic for "Until we dig again."

"ahthOOn SSyng!" Ogrese for "Much eating!"

"Aiiiee ooo (*howl*) bek aaau!" Abdegi for "I miss you already!"

"Porr ol pess waddo." Elfian for "Walk in the shade."

I memorized the sight of the birds and Simon. "Good-bye," I called. He waved.

Lest they be frightened out of their feathers, a garden separated the birds from the ogres. We passed beds of flowers while I tried to teach Char a few of the words he'd just heard. His memory was good, but his accent was unalterably Kyrrian.

"If they heard me, the elves would never let me stand under a tree again."

"The gnomes would hit you over the head with a shovel."

"Would the ogres decide I was unworthy of consumption?"

We neared their hut. Even though they were locked in, soldiers were posted within arrow range. An ogre glared at us through a window.

Ogres weren't dangerous only because of their size and their cruelty. They knew your secrets just by looking at you, and they used their knowledge. When they wanted to be, they were irresistibly persuasive. By the end of an ogre's first sentence in Kyrrian, you forgot his pointy teeth, the dried blood under his fingernails, and the coarse black hair that grew on his face in clumps. He became handsome in your eyes, and you thought him your best friend. By the end of the second sentence, you were so won over that he could do whatever he wanted with you, drop you in a pot to cook, or, if he was in a hurry, eat you raw.

“,pwich aooyeh zchoaK” a soft, lisping voice said.

“Did you hear that?” I asked.

“Doesn’t sound like an ogre. Where did it come from?”

“,pwich aooyeh zchoaK” the voice repeated, this time with a hint of tears in its tones.

A toddler gnome poked his head out of an aqueduct only a few feet from the hut. I saw him at the same moment the ogre did.

He could reach the child through the unglazed window! I started for the boy, but Char was quicker. He snatched him up just before the ogre’s arm shot out. Char backed away, holding the youngster, who squirmed to get out of his grasp.

“Give him to me,” I said, thinking I might be able to quiet him.

Char handed him over.

“szEE frah myNN,” the ogre hissed, glaring at Char. “myNN SSyng szEE. myNN thOOsh forns.” Then he turned to me and his expression changed. He started laughing. “mmeu ngah suSS hijyNN eMMong. myNN whadz szEE uiv. szEE AAh ohrth hahj ethSSif szEE.” Tears of mirth streaked down his cheeks, leaving trails on his filthy face.

Then he said in Kyrrian, not bothering to make his voice persuasive, “Come to me and bring the child.”

I stood my ground. Now I had to break the curse. My life and another’s depended on it.

My knees began to tremble from the need to walk. I held back, and my muscles cramped, shooting pain through my calves. I squeezed the little gnome in my effort to resist, and he yelped and twisted in my arms.

The ogre continued to laugh. Then he spoke again. "Obey me this instant. Come. Now."

Against my will I took a step. I stopped, and the trembling started again. Another step. And another. I saw nothing, except that leering face, looming closer and closer.

CHAPTER SEVEN

"Where are you going?" Char cried.

He could see where I was going. "I must," I said.

"Stop! I command you to stop."

I stopped and stood shaking, while soldiers crowded around the hut. Their swords pointed at the ogre, who glared at me, then turned his back and retreated into the dim interior.

"Why did you listen to him?" Char asked.

I was still having trouble with the child. He was pulling his little beard and wriggling to escape.

",pwich azzoogh fraecH" he cried.

I used his distress to avoid answering the question. "He's frightened."

But Char wasn't distracted. "Why did you listen to him, Ella?"

I had to answer, somehow. "His eyes," I lied. "Something about them. I had to do what he wanted."

"Have they found a new way to bewitch us?" Char sounded alarmed. "I must tell my father."

The gnome child wailed, thrashing at the air.

I wondered if the parrot's words might soothe him. I spoke them, hoping they weren't an insult. ".fwthchor evtoogh brzzay eerth ymmadboech evtoogh brzzaY"

The child's face cleared, and he smiled, showing pearly baby teeth. ",fwthchor evtoogh brzzay eerth ymmadboech evtoogh brzzaY" he repeated. There was a dimple in the folds of wrinkles and baby fat.

I put him down, and he took my hand and Char's.

"His parents must be worried," I said. I didn't know how to ask him where they were, and he was probably too young to answer.

They weren't by the ferocious beasts or by the grazing animals. At last, we spied an ancient female gnome sitting on the ground near the pond. Her head was between her knees, an image of defeat. Other gnomes searched the reeds and hedges or questioned passersby.

"!fraechramM" the little gnome called, pulling at Char and me.

The old gnome looked up, her face wet with tears. "!zhulpH" She grabbed him in a tight hug and covered his face and beard with kisses. Then she peered at us and recognized Char.

"Highness, thank you for the return of my grandson."

Char coughed, an embarrassed sound. "We're glad to bring him back, madam," he said. "He was almost an ogre's lunch."

"Char—Prince Charmont—saved him," I said. And saved me too.

"You have the gratitude of the gnomes." The gnome bowed her head. "I am zhatapH."

Hardly taller than I, she was much wider—not stout, but wide, which is the direction gnomes grow after they reach adulthood. She was the most dignified personage I had ever seen, and the oldest (except for Mandy probably). Her wrinkles had wrinkles, small folds in deeper folds of leathery skin. Her eyes were deep set and their copper color was clouded.

I curtsied, and wobbled. "I'm Ella," I said.

More gnomes came, and we were surrounded.

"How did you persuade him to come with you?" zhatapH asked. "He would not go with most humans."

"Ella spoke to him," Char said, sounding proud of me.

"What did you say?"

I hesitated. It was one thing to imitate parrots for Simon or to speak to a baby. It was another to sound like a fool in front of this stately lady. ",fwthchor evtoogh brzzay eerth ymmadboech evtoogh brzzaY" I said finally.

"No wonder he came with you," zhatapH said.

"!fraecH" zhulpH cried joyously. He squirmed in her arms.

A younger gnome woman took the child. "Where did you learn to speak Gnomic?" she asked. "I am zhulpH's mother."

I explained about the parrots. "What did I say to zhulpH?"

"It is an expression. We say it as a greeting," zhatapH said. "In Kyrrian it is 'Digging is good for the wealth and good for the health.'" She held her hand out to me. "zhulpH is not the only one you will save. I see it."

What else could she see? Mandy had said a few gnomes could tell the future. "Can you see what's ahead for me?"

"Gnomes do not see detail. What you will wear

tomorrow, what you will say, are mysteries. I see outlines only."

"What are they?"

"Danger, a quest, three figures. They are close to you, but they are not your friends." She let my hand go. "Beware of them!"

On our way out of the menagerie, Char said, "Tonight I shall triple the guard around the ogres. And soon I shall catch a centaur and give it to you."

Dame Olga was punctual. She and her daughters watched while my trunk and a barrel of Tonic were loaded on top of the coach.

Father was there to see me off, and Mandy stood at a distance.

"How few things you have," Hattie told me.

Dame Olga agreed. "Ella is not outfitted in accordance with her station, Sir Peter. My girls have eight trunks between them."

"Hattie has five and a half trunks, Mother. And I have only—" Olive stopped speaking to count on her fingers. "Less. I have less, and it's not fair."

Father cut in smoothly. "It's most kind of you to take Ella with you, Dame Olga. I only hope she won't be a bother."

"Oh, she won't bother me, Sir P. I'm not going."

Father winced at the abbreviation.

Dame Olga continued, "With a coachman and two footmen, they will be safe from everything except ogres. And from ogres I could offer little protection. Besides, they'll have more fun without their old mother."

After a pause, Father said, "Not old. Never old,

madam." He turned to me. "I wish you a comfortable journey, child." He kissed my cheek. "I'll miss you."

Liar.

A footman opened the coach door. Hattie and Olive were handed in. I ran to Mandy. I couldn't leave without a last hug.

"Make them all disappear. Please," I whispered.

"Oh, Ella, sweetie. You'll be fine." She clasped me hard.

"Eleanor, your friends are waiting," Father called.

I climbed into the coach, stowing a small carpetbag in a corner, and we started to move. For comfort I touched my chest where Mother's necklace was concealed. If she were alive, I wouldn't be rolling away from home in the company of these creatures.

"I would never embrace a cook." Hattie shuddered.

"No," I agreed. "What cook would let you?"

Hattie returned to an earlier subject. "With so few belongings, the other girls will hardly know whether you are a servant or one of us."

"Why does your gown pucker in front?" Olive asked.

"Is that a necklace? Why wear it under your clothes?" Hattie asked.

"Is it ugly?" Olive said. "Is that why you hide it?"

"It's not ugly."

"Show it to us. Ollie and I so want to see it."

An order. I brought it out. It didn't matter here. There were no thieves to steal it.

"Ooooh," Olive said. "It's even nicer than Mama's best chain."

"No one would think you were a servant with that. It's very fine. Although it's much too long for you."

Hattie fingered the silver ropes. "Olive, see how milky the pearls are."

Olive's fingers joined Hattie's.

"Let go!" I shifted out of their reach.

"We wouldn't hurt it. May I try it on? Mother lets me try on her necklaces and I never hurt them."

"No, you can't."

"Oh, let me. There's a dear."

An order. "Do I have to?" I asked. It slipped out. I could have swallowed my tongue.

Hattie's eyes glittered. "Yes, you have to. Give it over."

"Just for a minute," I said, unclasping it. I didn't delay. They mustn't see me struggle against the curse.

"Fasten it around my neck . . ."

I did so.

". . . Olive."

The order had been for her sister.

"Thank you, my dear." Hattie settled back in her seat. "I was born to wear jewels like this."

"Let me try it, Ella," Olive said.

"When you're older," Hattie answered.

But I had to obey. I tried desperately to ignore Olive's order, but all my complaints started: churning stomach, pounding temples, shortness of breath.

"Let her have her turn," I said through clenched teeth.

"See," Olive said. "Ella says I can."

"I know what's best for you, Olive. You and Ella are both too young—"

I lunged at her and unfastened the necklace before she had time to stop me.

"Don't give it to her, Ella," Hattie said. "Return it to me."

I did.

"Give it to me, Ella," Olive said, her voice rising. "Don't be so mean, Hattie."

I snatched the necklace back from Hattie and passed it to Olive.

Hattie stared at me. I could see her start to work out what had happened.

"Mother wore that necklace to her wedding," I said, hoping to deflect her thoughts. "And her mother . . ."

"Are you always so obedient, Ella? Return the necklace to me."

"I won't let her," Olive said.

"Yes you will, or I'll see that you get no dinner tonight."

I took the necklace away from Olive. Hattie fastened it around her neck and patted it complacently. "Ella, you should give it to me. It would be a token of our friendship."

"We're not friends."

"Yes we are. I'm devoted to you. Olive likes you too, don't you, Ollie?"

Olive nodded solemnly.

"I believe you will give it to me if I say you must. Do so, Ella, for friendship's sake. You must."

No, I wouldn't. She couldn't have it. "You can have it." The words burst from me.

"Thank you. What a generous friend we have, Olive." She changed the subject. "The servants were careless when they cleaned the coach. That dust ball is a disgrace. We shouldn't have to ride in such filth. Pick it up, Ella."

An order I liked. I grabbed the dust and ground it into her face. "It becomes you," I said.

But the satisfaction was fleeting.

CHAPTER EIGHT

Hattie didn't know about Lucinda and the curse, but she understood I always had to follow her orders. After I rubbed dust in her face, all she did was smile. The smile meant that dust weighed little in the balance of her power.

I retreated to a corner of the coach and gazed out the window.

Hattie hadn't ordered me not to take the necklace back again. What if I lifted it over her large head? Or what if I yanked it off her neck? It would be better broken than owned by her.

I tried. I told my arms to move, told my hands to grasp. But the curse wouldn't let me. If someone else had ordered me to take it back, I would have had to. But I couldn't will myself to reclaim it. So I made myself look at it, to become accustomed to the sight. While I stared, Hattie stroked the chain, gloating.

In a few minutes her eyes closed. Her mouth fell open, and she began to snore.

Olive crossed the carriage to sit next to me. "I want a present to show we're friends too," she said.

"Why don't you give me a gift instead?"

The furrows in her forehead deepened. "No. You give me."

An order. "What would you like?" I asked.

"I want money. Give me money."

As he'd promised, Father had given me a purse of silver KJs. I reached into my carpetbag and pulled out a coin. "Here you are. Now we're friends."

She spat on the coin and rubbed it to make it shine. "We're friends," she agreed. She crossed back to her former seat and brought the coin close to her eyes to study it.

I looked at the snoring Hattie. She was probably dreaming of ways to order me about. I looked at Olive, who was running the edge of the KJ over her forehead and down her nose. I began to long for finishing school. At least there they wouldn't be my only companions.

In a few minutes Olive joined Hattie in slumber. When I was certain both of them were soundly asleep, I dared to fetch Mandy's other present, the book of fairy tales, out of my bag. I turned away from the two of them, to hide the book and to catch the light from the carriage window.

When I opened it, instead of a fairy tale, I found an illustration of Mandy! She was dicing a turnip. Next to the turnip was the chicken I had watched her pluck that morning. She was crying. I had suspected she was fighting back tears when she hugged me.

The page blurred because my eyes filled with tears too. But I refused to cry in front of Hattie and Olive, even if they were asleep.

If Mandy had been in the coach with me, she would have hugged me and I could have cried as long as I liked. She would have patted my back and told me—

No. Those thoughts would make me cry. If Mandy

were here, she'd tell me why it would be big, bad magic to turn Hattie into a rabbit. And I'd wonder again what fairies were good for.

That helped. I checked to make sure they were still sleeping; then I examined the next page. It showed a room that probably was in King Jerrold's castle, because Char was there and the crest of Kyrria was painted on the wall above a tapestry. Char was talking to three of the soldiers who had been in the ogres' guard at the menagerie.

I puzzled about the meaning. Maybe an explanation would follow. I turned the page and found two more illustrations, neither one of Char or soldiers.

On the verso was a map of Frell. There was our manor, bearing the legend, "Sir Peter of Frell." My fingers traced the route to the old castle and on to the menagerie. There was the south road out of Frell, the road we were on now, far beyond the map's boundaries, far beyond the manor of Sir Peter of Frell.

The right-hand illustration showed Father's coach, followed by three mule-drawn wagons loaded with goods for trade. Father sat atop the coach with the driver, who was plying his whip. Father leaned into the wind and grinned.

What would the book show me next?

A real fairy tale this time, "The Shoemaker and the Elves." In this version, though, each elf had a personality, and I came to know them better than the shoemaker. And I finally understood why the elves disappeared after the shoemaker made clothes for them. They went away to help a giant rid herself of a swarm of mosquitoes, too small for her to see. Although the elves left a thank-you note for the shoemaker, he put his coffee cup down on it, and it stuck to the cup's damp bottom.

The story made sense now.

"Your book must be fascinating. Let me see it," Hattie said.

I jumped. If she took this from me too, I'd kill her. The book got heavier as I handed it over.

Her eyes widened as she read. "You enjoy this? 'The Life Cycle of the Centaur Tick'?" She turned pages. " 'Gnomish Silver Mining in Hazardous Terrain'?"

"Isn't it interesting?" I said, my panic subsiding. "You can read for a while. If we're going to be friends, we should have the same interests."

"You can share *my* interests, dear." She returned the book.

Our journey taught me what to expect from Hattie.

At the inn on our first night, she informed me I had taken the space in their carriage that would otherwise have been occupied by their maid.

"But we shan't suffer, because you can take her place." She cocked her head to one side. "No, you are almost noble. It would be an insult to make a servant of you. You will be my lady-in-waiting, and I shall share you with my sister sometimes. Ollie, is there something Ella can do to help you?"

"No! I can dress and undress myself," Olive said defiantly.

"No one said you can't." Hattie sat on the bed we were all to share. She lifted her feet. "Kneel down and take my slippers off for me, Ella. My toes ache."

Without comment I removed them. My nose filled

with the ripe smell of her feet. I carried the slippers to the window and tossed them out.

Hattie yawned. "You've only made extra work for yourself. Go down and fetch them."

Olive rushed to the window. "Your slippers fell into a bucket of slops!"

I had to carry the stinking slippers back to our room, but Hattie had to wear them until she was able to get fresh ones from her trunk. After that, she thought more carefully about her commands.

At breakfast the next morning she pronounced the porridge inedible. "Don't eat it, Ella. It will make you sick." She loaded her spoon with oatmeal.

Steam rose from the bowl before me, and I caught the scent of cinnamon. Mandy always put cinnamon in her porridge too.

"Why are you eating it if it's bad?" Olive asked her sister. "I'm hungry."

"Yours looks all right. I'm eating mine even though it's vile"—her tongue licked a speck of cereal off the corner of her mouth—"because I need nourishment to take charge on our journey."

"You're not in ch—" Olive began.

"You don't fancy your porridge, miss?" The innkeeper sounded worried.

"My sister's stomach is queasy," Hattie said. "You may take her bowl away."

"I'm not her sister," I said as the innkeeper disappeared into the kitchen.

Hattie laughed, scraping her spoon around her empty bowl for the last remnants of porridge.

The innkeeper was back with a plate of thick brown

bread studded with nuts and raisins. "Perhaps this will tempt the lass's stomach," he said.

I managed to take a big bite before a lady at the next table called him away.

"Put it down, Ella." Hattie broke off a corner of the bread and tasted it. "It's much too rich."

"Rich food is good for me," Olive said, reaching across the table.

Between them my breakfast disappeared in four bites.

That swallow of bread was the last food I had on our three-day trip, except for Tonic. Hattie would have deprived me of it too, except she sampled it first. And then I relished her nauseated expression when she swallowed.

CHAPTER NINE

We passed through rich farmland on the final day of our journey to Jenn, the town where our finishing school was located. The day was hazy and warm, and I was almost too hot to be hungry. Hattie had energy for only one command: to fan her.

"Fan me too," Olive said. She had worked out that if Hattie told me to do something, I would do it, and if she directed me to do the same thing, I would do that too. Hattie hadn't explained my obedience to her. She didn't bother to explain much to the slow-thinking Olive, and she must have enjoyed keeping the delicious secret to herself.

My arms ached. My stomach rumbled. I stared out the window at a flock of sheep and wished for a diversion that would take my mind away from lamb and lentil salad. My wish was granted instantly as the coach took off in a mad gallop.

"Ogres!" the coachman yelled. A cloud of dust hid the road behind us. Through it I made out a band of ogres, kicking up the dust as they chased us.

But we were outdistancing them. The cloud was receding.

"Why do you run from your friends?" one of them called. It was the sweetest voice I had ever heard. "We bear gifts of your hearts' desires. Riches, love, eternal life . . ."

Heart's desire. Mother! The ogres would bring her back from death. Why were we tearing away from everything we most wanted?

"Slow down," Hattie ordered unnecessarily. The coachman had already reined in the horses.

The ogres were only yards behind. Untouched by their magic, the sheep were *baa*-ing and bleating their fear. Briefly their noise covered the honeyed words and the spell broke. I remembered that the ogres couldn't revive Mother. The horses were again whipped to a gallop.

But the ogres would be beyond the sheep in a minute and we'd be at their mercy again. I shouted to Hattie and Olive and to the coachman and footmen. "Yell so you can't hear them."

The coachman understood first and joined my voice with his, shouting words I'd never heard before. Then Hattie began. "Eat me last! Eat me last!" she shrieked.

But it was Olive who saved us. Her wordless roar drowned out thought. I don't know how she drew breath; the sound was unending. It continued as we passed the outlying homes of Jenn, while the ogres faded from sight and while I recovered from my fright.

"Quiet, Ollie," Hattie said. "Nobody is going to be eaten. You're giving me a headache."

But Olive didn't hush until the coachman stopped the carriage, came inside with us, and slapped her smartly across the face.

"Sorry, miss," he said, and popped back out.

ஐ

Finishing school was in an ordinary wooden house. Except for its enormous ornamental shrubs pruned into the shapes of wide-skirted maidens, it might have been the home of any not-so-prosperous merchant.

I hoped the lunch portions were generous.

The door opened as we drove up, and an erect, gray-haired lady strutted down the walkway to our carriage.

"Welcome, young ladies." She swept into the smoothest curtsy I'd ever seen. We curtsied in return.

She waved a hand at me. "But who is this?"

I spoke quickly, before Hattie could explain me in a way I didn't want to be explained.

"I'm Ella, madam. My father is Sir Peter of Frell. He wrote a letter." From my carpetbag I extracted Father's letter and the purse he'd given me.

She tucked the letter and the purse (after weighing it expertly in her palm) into her apron pocket.

"What a lovely surprise. I am Madame Edith, headmistress of your new home. Welcome to our humble establishment." She curtsied again.

I wished she'd stop. My right knee cracked when I went down.

"We just had lunch."

So much for generous portions.

"And we are sitting down to our embroidery. The young ladies are anxious to meet you, and it's never too soon to start being finished."

She ushered us into a large sunny room. "Young ladies," she announced, "here are three new friends for you."

A roomful of maidens rose, curtsied, then resumed

their seats. Each one wore a pink gown with a yellow hair ribbon. My gown was stained and wrinkled from the journey, and my hair was probably limp and unkempt.

"Back to work, ladies," Madame Edith said. "Sewing Mistress will help the new pupils."

I lowered myself into a chair near the door and stared defiantly at the elegance around me. I met the eyes of a girl about my age. She smiled hesitantly. Maybe my look softened, because her smile grew and she winked.

Sewing Mistress approached, bearing a needle, an assortment of colored thread, and a round of white linen marked with a design of flowers. I was to follow the outline and stitch the flowers in thread. The cloth could then cover a pillow or the back of a chair.

After she explained what to do, Sewing Mistress left me, assuming I would know how to do it. But I had never before held a needle. Although I watched the other girls, I could not thread it. I struggled for a quarter hour till Sewing Mistress rushed to my side. "The child has been raised by ogres or worse!" she exclaimed, snatching it away from me. "Hold it delicately. It's not a spear. One brings the thread to it." She threaded the needle with green thread and returned it to me.

I held it delicately, as ordered.

She left my side, and I stared stupidly at my task. Then I stuck the needle into the outline of a rose. My head ached from lack of food.

"You have to knot the end of the thread and start underneath." The speaker was the lass who had winked at me. She had pulled her chair next to mine. "And Sewing Mistress will ridicule you if you sew a green rose. Roses have to be red or pink, or yellow if you're daring."

A pink gown similar to the one she wore was spread across her lap. She bent her head over it to make a tiny stitch.

Her dark hair was plaited into many braids that were gathered and woven into a knot high on her head. Her skin was the color of cinnamon with a tint of raspberry in her cheeks (I couldn't help thinking of food). Her lips curved up naturally, giving her a pleased and contented air.

Her name was Areida, and her family lived in Amonta, a city just over the border in Ayortha. She spoke with an Ayorthaian accent, smacking her lips after the letter *m* and pronouncing her *l*'s as *y*'s.

"Abensa utyu anja ubensu." I hoped this was Ayorthaian for "I'm pleased to meet you." I had learned it from a parrot.

She smiled at me ecstatically. "Ubensu ockommo Ayortha?"

"I only know a few words," I confessed.

She was miserably disappointed. "It would have been so nice to have someone to talk to in my language."

"You could teach me."

"Your accent is good," she said doubtfully. "But Writing Mistress teaches Ayorthaian to everyone, and no one has picked it up at all."

"I have a knack for languages."

She started to teach me right then. Once heard, always remembered is the way with languages and me. By the end of an hour I was forming short sentences. Areida was delighted.

"Utyu ubensu evtame oyjento?" I asked. ("Do you like finishing school?")

She shrugged.

"You don't? Is it terrible?" I asked, reverting to Kyrrian.

A shadow fell across my neglected sewing. Sewing Mistress picked up my pillow cover and announced dramatically, "Three stitches in all this time. Three vast, messy stitches. Like three teeth in a toothless gum. Go to your room and stay there until it is time for bed. No supper for you tonight."

My stomach growled so loudly that the whole room must have heard it. Hattie smirked at me. She couldn't have planned better herself.

I wouldn't add to her pleasure. "I'm not hungry," I announced.

"Then you may do without breakfast as well, for your impertinence."

CHAPTER TEN

A maid showed me to a corridor lined with doors. Each one was painted a different pastel color and had a card affixed to it announcing the name of the room. We passed the Lime Room, the Daisy Room, and the Opal Room and stopped before the Lavender Room. The maid opened the door.

For a moment I forgot my hunger. I was in a cloud of light purple. Some of the purples blushed faintly pink, others were tinted pale blue, but there was no other color.

The curtains were streamers, undulating from the breeze made by the door closing behind me. Beneath my feet was a hooked rug in the design of a huge violet. In a corner stood a clay chamber pot, disguised as a decorative cabbage. The five beds were swathed in a gauzy fabric. The five bureaus were painted with wavy stripes of pale and paler lavender.

I wanted to throw myself on a bed and cry about being so hungry and about everything else, but these were not beds onto which one could throw oneself. A purple chair was placed next to one of the two windows. I sank into it.

If I didn't succumb to starvation, I would be here for a long time, with hateful mistresses and with Hattie ordering me about. I stared out the window at Madame Edith's garden until exhaustion and hunger produced a kind of stupor in me. In a while, I slept.

"Here, Ella. You can eat this."

An urgent whisper pushed its way into my dream about roasted pheasant stuffed with chestnuts.

Someone shook my shoulder. "Wake up. Ella, wake up."

An order. I was awake.

Areida thrust a roll into my hands. "It's all I could get. Eat it before the others come in."

In two swallows I ate the soft white roll, more air than sustenance. But more sustenance than I'd had in days.

"Thank you. Do you sleep in here too?"

She nodded.

"Where?"

The door opened and three maidens entered.

"Look! Queer ducks flock together." The speaker was the tallest pupil in the school. She pronounced her *l*'s as *y*'s, mocking Areida's accent.

"Ecete iffibensi asura edanse evtame oyjento?" I asked Areida. ("Is this how they behave at finishing school?")

"Otemso iffibensi asura ippiri." ("Sometimes they are much worse.")

"Are you from Ayortha too?" the tall maiden asked me.

"No, but Areida is teaching me the beautiful Ayorthaian language. In Ayorthaian, you are an 'ibwi unju.'" It only meant "tall girl." I didn't know any insults in Ayorthaian. However, Areida was laughing, which made it seem the worst of epithets.

I laughed too. Areida collapsed on top of me, and together we shook the purple chair.

Madame Edith, the headmistress, bustled in. "Young ladies! What do I see?"

Areida leaped up, but I remained seated. I couldn't stop laughing.

"My chairs are not made to take such abuse. And young ladies do not sit two to a seat. Do you hear me? Ella! Stop your unseemly laughter."

I stopped mid giggle.

"That's better. Since it's your first day here, I shall excuse your behavior and trust that it will have improved tomorrow." Madame Edith turned to the others. "Into your nightdresses, young ladies. The Shores of Sleep are approaching."

Areida and I exchanged glances. It was very cheering to have a friend.

Everyone else reached the Shores of Sleep, but I remained oceans away. I had been given a nightdress so covered with bows and frills that I couldn't lie flat comfortably.

I slipped out of bed and opened my carpetbag. If I couldn't sleep, I could read. Madame Edith thought fear of the dark was to be expected in young ladies, so a lamp was left burning.

My book opened to a letter from Mandy.

Dear Ella,

This morning I baked scones. Bertha and Nathan and I will eat them for a snack before we go to bed. But I baked two extra. We'll have to divide yours and eat them too.

I promised myself I wouldn't trouble you by saying how much I miss you, and see how I start.

That parrot man, name of Simon, came here today with one of his birds to give you. It speaks Gnomic and Elfian. He said it wasn't fine enough for the menagerie, but you might like it. He told me what to feed it. I never thought I'd be cook to a parrot.

I wish it would stop talking once in a while. I wonder if I have a recipe for parrot stew. Don't worry, sweet, I would never cook your present.

Yesterday, you had a grander visitor, and received a bigger gift than a bird. The prince himself came to see you, leading a centaur colt. When I told him you were away from home, he wanted to know where you'd gone and when you'd be back. And when he heard you were at finishing school, he was indignant. He demanded to know why you needed to be finished since there was nothing wrong with you to start with. I couldn't answer him because I'd like to ask that father of yours the same question.

I did tell him we had nowhere to keep a growing centaur. He's a little beauty, but what can I do with him? Your prince said he'd raise him for you. He asked me to tell you the colt's name, Apple. That made me remember my manners, and I gave him his name to eat before he left with the prince.

Speaking of leaving, your father departed the same day you did. Said he was off to the greenies, which I gathered was his disrespectful name for the elves. Said not to expect him back anytime soon.

I wish you were coming home soon. Bertha and

Nathan send their love, and I send mine, by the bushel, by the barrel, by the tun.

From your old cook,
Mandy

P.S. Drink your Tonic.

I closed the book, and whispered to its spine, "Don't erase the letter, please." Then I drank my Tonic.

A centaur colt! A little beauty. If only I could see him, and pet him, and let him know me.

The tears that hadn't come in the afternoon came now. Mandy would be desperate if she knew I hadn't eaten in three days and if she knew I was under the thumb of a monster like Hattie.

The next morning, Music Mistress led us in song, and singled out my off-key voice.

"Ella does not notice that there is more than one note," she told everyone. "Come here, child. Sing this." She played a note on the harpsichord.

I wouldn't be able to. I could never carry a tune. What would happen when I couldn't obey?

I sang the wrong note. Music Mistress frowned.

"Higher, or we shall send you to a different school to sing with the young gentlemen." She depressed the key again.

My next attempt was much too high. One lass covered her ears. I wished her an earache.

Music Mistress played again.

My temples throbbed. I sang.

"A little lower."

I hit the note. She played another. I sang it. She

played a scale. I sang every note. I beamed. I'd always wished I could sing. I sang the scale again, louder. Perfect!

"That's enough, young lady. You must sing when I tell you to, and not otherwise."

An hour later Dancing Mistress told me to step lightly.

My partner was Julia, the tall maiden who had teased Areida the night before. I pressed on her arms, using her to support my weight so I could step lightly.

"Stop that." She pulled away.

I fell. I heard giggles.

Dancing Mistress took Julia's place. I couldn't lean on her. I pretended my feet were balloons. I pretended the floor would crack if I didn't move lightly. We stepped. We glided. We sprang forward, jumped back. I wasn't graceful, but I didn't shake the ground. My gown was soaked with perspiration.

"That's better."

At lunch Manners Mistress said, "Don't rap your knuckles on the table, Ella. The king would be ashamed of you." She frequently invoked King Jerrold.

Tables were forever safe from me.

"Take small stitches, Eleanor, and don't yank the thread. It's not a rein, and you're not a coachman," Sewing Mistress said later in the afternoon.

I stabbed myself with the needle, but my stitches shrank.

It was the same every day. I dreaded new orders. The curse didn't make me change easily. I had to concentrate every second. In my mind, I repeated my commands in an endless refrain. When I awoke, I instructed myself not to bounce out of bed. Leave the nightdress for the servants to put away. At breakfast don't blow on my porridge, and don't spit out the lumps. On our afternoon walk, don't skip, don't leap about.

Once I actually spoke aloud. It was at dinner. "Don't slurp," I instructed myself. I said it softly, but a pupil seated near me heard, and she told the others.

The only subjects that came easily were those taught by Writing Mistress: composition and ciphering. She also taught penmanship, which was the one subject in which I did not attain excellence, because Writing Mistress issued no orders.

She taught Ayorthaian but no other languages. When I told her I knew a little of the exotic tongues and wished to learn more, she gave me a dictionary of exotic speech. It became my second-favorite book, after Mandy's present.

Whenever I had time, I practiced the languages, especially Ogrese. The meanings were dreadful, but there was an attraction in speaking the words. They were smooth, sleek, and slithery, the way a talking snake would sound. There were words like *psySSahbuSS* (delicious), *SSyng* (eat), *hijyNN* (dinner), *eFFuth* (taste), and *FFnOO* (sour).

My progress in all my subjects astounded the mistresses. In my first month I did little right. In my second I did little wrong. And gradually, it all became natural: light steps, small stitches, quiet voice, ramrod-straight back, deep curtsies without creaking knees, no yawns, soup tilted away from me, and no slurping.

But in bed, before I fell asleep, I'd imagine what I would do if I were free of Lucinda's curse. At dinner I'd paint lines of gravy on my face and hurl meat pasties at

Manners Mistress. I'd pile Headmistress's best china on my head and walk with a wobble and a swagger till every piece was smashed. Then I'd collect the smashed pottery and the smashed meat pasties and grind them into all my perfect stitchery.

CHAPTER ELEVEN

Except for Areida, I had little pleasure from the society at finishing school. Only Hattie's set pretended to be friendly, and they treated me with the same oily condescension Hattie visited on me in public. They were an odious group, Hattie and the two she called her special friends, Blossom and Delicia. Blossom was the niece and sole heir to an unmarried earl. Her conversation was mostly worries that the earl would marry and have a child who would replace her as his heir. Delicia, the daughter of a duke, spoke rarely. When she did, it was to complain. The room was too drafty; the meal was ill prepared; a housemaid had acted above her station; one of the other pupils wore rouge.

The mistresses came to dislike me too. At first, while I struggled to satisfy them and began to succeed, they made a pet of me, which I hated. But when "finished" behavior became my second nature, they learned I was nobody's pet. I spoke as infrequently as I could and met their eyes only when I had to. And I returned to my old game.

"Sing more softly, Ella. They can hear you in Ayortha."

I became inaudible.

"Not so soft. The rest of us would like to hear your sweet tones."

I sang too loud again, although not so much as before. Music Mistress had to spend a quarter hour inching me along to the desired volume.

"Lift your feet, young ladies. This is a spirited gavotte."

My leg shot up above my waist.

And so on. It was a tiresome game, but I had to play it or feel a complete puppet.

Hattie didn't tell anyone about my obedience. When she had an order for me, she'd tell me to meet her in the garden after supper when no one else was near. On the first such occasion, she instructed me to pick a bouquet for her.

Luckily, she didn't know I was goddaughter to a fairy cook. I picked the most fragrant blooms, then ran to the herb garden hoping to find something useful. Effelwort was my preference. If I found it, Hattie would have an itchy rash on her face for a week.

Most of the herbs were the ordinary sort, but as I turned to leave, I spotted a sprig of bogweed. Taking care not to breathe its scent, I plucked it and placed it next to a rose.

Hattie was delighted with the flowers and buried her face in them. "They're sublime. But what . . . ?" As the scent of the bogweed worked on her, her smile faded, and her expression became vacant.

"What would make you stop giving me orders?"

She answered in a flat voice, "If you stopped obeying them."

Of course. I had wasted a question and I had no idea how long the bogweed scent would last. But as long as it lasted, I could ask her anything and she would answer honestly.

"What else would stop you?" I asked quickly.

"Nothing." She thought. "My death."

No likely release from that quarter. "What orders do you plan to give me?"

"I don't plan."

"Why do you hate me?"

"You never admired me."

"Do you admire me?"

"Yes."

"Why?"

"You're pretty. And brave."

She envied me. I was amazed. "What do you fear?" I asked.

"Ogres. Bandits. Drowning. Becoming ill. Climbing mountains. Mice. Dogs. Cats. Birds. Horses. Spiders. Worms. Tunnels. Poi—"

I stopped her. She was afraid of everything. "What do you want most in the world?"

"To be queen."

A rabbit queen. Only I would obey her.

Her face was changing, resuming its usual expression of gleeful malice. I tried one more question. "What are your secrets?"

She didn't answer, just tugged cruelly on a handful of my hair. Her eyes lost their dull cast.

"Why am I standing here?" She looked down at her flowers but didn't sniff them again. "Oh, yes. What a good lady-in-waiting to bring me such a beautiful bouquet." She frowned. "But one scent is not sweet. Take it out."

I removed the bogweed and ground it under my foot. If I had thought of it, I could have asked her how she could be defeated.

Hattie's orders were chiefly chores. I think she lacked the imagination to devise more interesting commands. I brushed her clothes, cleaned her boots, rubbed her neck where it ached. Several times I had to sneak into the pantry and steal cookies. On one occasion I had to clip her toenails.

"Do you rub brine into your feet?" I asked, trying not to choke.

I took revenge whenever I could. Spiders and mice from Madame Edith's cellar found their way into Hattie's bed. I'd stay awake at night and wait for the satisfying shriek.

And so it went. Hattie issued commands and I retaliated. But there was no balance. Hattie was always ahead. She had the power. She held the whip.

Areida was my only comfort. We ate our meals side by side. We sewed together. In our dancing lessons, we were partners. I told her about Frell and Mandy and Char. She told me about her parents, who kept an inn. They weren't wealthy, another reason she was unpopular. When she left school, she would use her accomplishments to help them.

She was kinder than anyone I'd ever known. When Julia, the tall wench, ate too many grapes from Madame Edith's arbor and was sick all night, Areida nursed her, although Julia's friends slept soundly. I helped, but only for Areida's sake. My nature was not so forgiving.

In the garden one evening, I found myself telling Areida about Mother.

"Before she died, we used to climb trees like this one." I rested a hand on the trunk of a low-branching oak. "We'd go way up and sit as quiet as could be. Then we'd toss twigs or acorns at anyone who passed beneath."

"What happened to her?" she asked. "Don't tell me if you don't want to."

I didn't mind. When I finished telling her, she sang an Ayorthaian mourning song.

"Hard farewell,
With no greeting to come.
Sad farewell,
When love is torn away.
Long farewell,
Till Death dies.

"But the lost one is with you.
Her tenderness strengthens you,
Her gaiety uplifts you,
Her honor purifies you.
More than memory,
The lost one is found."

Areida's voice was as smooth as syrup and as rich as gnomes' gold. I cried, steady tears, like rain. And, like rain, they brought ease.

"You have a beautiful voice," I said when I could speak.

"We Ayorthaians are all singers, but Singing Mistress says my voice is too husky."

"Hers is thin as a string. And yours is perfect."

A bell rang in the house, calling us in to prepare for bed.

"Is my nose red from crying?" I asked.

"A little."

"I don't want Ha— the others to see. I'll stay out awhile longer."

"Manners Mistress will be angry."

I shrugged. "She'll only tell me I've disgraced the king."

"I'll stay with you. I can watch your nose and tell you when it's not red anymore."

"Pay attention. Don't let your eyes wander." I wrinkled the feature.

Areida giggled. "I won't."

"Manners Mistress will ask what we're doing out here." I was laughing too.

"I'll tell her I'm watching your nose."

"And I'll tell her I'm wrinkling it."

"She'll want to know what the king would think of our behavior."

"I'll tell her the queen watches every night while he wrinkles his nose seven times."

The bell rang again.

"Your nose isn't red now," Areida said.

We ran for the house and met Manners Mistress at the door, on her way to search for us. The sight of her set us off again.

"Young ladies! Go to your room. What would the king say?"

In the hall, still giggling, we met Hattie.

"Having a nice time?"

"We were," I answered.

"I won't keep you then, but tomorrow, Ella, you must spend some time in the garden with me."

"You shouldn't associate with the lower orders, like that wench from Ayortha," she said the next evening.

"Areida is a higher order than you are, and I choose my own friends."

"My dear, my dear. I hate to cause you grief, but you must end your friendship with her."

CHAPTER TWELVE

Hattie returned to the house, but I stayed outside. I watched her leave, hating her way of walking—a mince combined with a waddle. She stopped to pick a flower and lift it to her nose, posturing for me.

I sat on a bench and stared down at the pebbled walk. In all the times I'd imagined the miseries she could inflict on me, I'd never imagined this. I'd thought of injuries, and I'd imagined terrible embarrassment, but I'd never thought of this kind of hurt.

Areida was in our room now, waiting to give me a lesson in Ayorthaian. I remained seated. I couldn't face her.

Was there a way to stop being her friend without hurting her? I could pretend I had suddenly become mute so I wouldn't be able to talk to her. But in that circumstance she'd be my friend as much as ever. She'd talk to me, and we'd invent a sign language, which would be great fun. And that wouldn't be ending our friendship, so the curse wouldn't let me do it. Besides, a mistress would be sure to say, "Speak, Ella," and I would have to.

I could announce I'd taken a vow of loneliness. But Areida would be hurt that I'd taken such a vow.

If only Mother hadn't forbidden me to tell about the

curse. But then again, explaining would be an act of friendship, which the curse also wouldn't allow.

The bell rang calling us to bed. I was late again, but tonight there was no Areida to joke with about our tardiness.

In our room, she sat on my bed, completing a letter for Writing Mistress.

"Where were you? I've been reviewing the imperative."

"I'm tired," I said, not answering the question.

Perhaps I did look tired, or troubled, because she didn't press me. She only patted my arm and said, "We can study imperatives tomorrow."

In bed, I didn't want to sleep. I wanted to savor the last few hours before I had to hurt her.

Sleep on, Areida. Be my friend for one more night.

A long vigil lay ahead. I pulled out my magic book. It opened to a letter from Dame Olga to her daughters.

My sweet darlings,

Your poor mother is desolate without you.

I attended a cotillion last night at the palace. I wore my wine-colored taffeta gown and my ruby pendant. But it was for naught. The company was thin because King Jerrold is away, although Prince Charmont was there. That charming man, Sir Peter, wasn't there either. I was desolate. I understand he is off traveling and becoming richer, I imagine. I wish him well and will be first to pay my respects on his return.

Three pages followed describing Dame Olga's social

calendar and her wardrobe. In closing, she remembered she had daughters and was writing to them.

> *I hope both of you are eating well to keep up your strength. Olive, pray remember not to eat Madame Edith's flowers. If you were to sicken or die, I should be desolate. Hattie, I hope you have found a trustworthy servant to dress your hair. Madame E. promised it could be arranged.*
>
> *I expect the two of you are amazingly finished by now. But do not toil too hard, my dears. If you can sing and dance charmingly, eat daintily, and sew a little, you will be fine ladies and I shall be proud of you.*
>
> *My sweets, the carriage has arrived. I am in my lemon silk calling gown, and I must fly.*
>
> *Your adoring mother,*
> *Dame Olga*

Why was a trustworthy servant necessary to dress Hattie's hair? I compared the luxuriant tresses of Hattie and her mother with Olive's thin curls, and I remembered Hattie's attack on my hair after she smelled the bogweed. I laughed out loud. Hattie and Dame Olga wore wigs!

Thank you, Dame Olga. I hadn't expected to laugh tonight. I turned the page.

On the verso was an illustration of a centaur colt—Apple, I was sure—nuzzling a young man—Char. The colt *was* a beauty. His hide was deep brown with a tan mane and an irregular tan star on his chest. Skinny and leggy, he was made for speed, although he was too young to bear a rider. Would he ever really be mine?

On the right was a letter from Char to his father.

Dear Father,

I hope this finds you safe and well. My mother and my sister and brothers are in good health, as am I.

Since I received instructions to join you, I have been filled with gratitude for your confidence in me. The knights you have chosen to follow me are stout fellows and bear the command of a stripling with good humor. My mother worries, but I tell her they will not let harm befall me.

In truth, Father, I am so stirred up by the thought of my first military duty—even if it is only reviewing border troops—that I hardly hear my good mother. Who knows? Perhaps the ogres will raid and there will be a skirmish. I do not fear injury, only that I may not acquit myself well.

Skirmishes with ogres! How could there not be danger?

Char continued to describe the visit of a trade delegation and the same ball that Dame Olga had attended, although he didn't mention what he had worn.

Near the bottom of the page, my name appeared.

I am training a centaur colt for a lass I know. Her mother was the late Lady Eleanor. I admire the daughter, Ella, but she has gone to finishing school, where I fear she will be made less admirable. What do they teach in such places? Sewing and curtsying? It is a great distance to go to learn such paltry tricks.

Would he stop liking me now that I was no longer clumsy? I had never enjoyed being a small elephant and hadn't mourned the loss till now.

Would he even be alive to stop liking me, or would he be an ogre's lunch?

The next page was a letter from Father to his bailiff.

Dear James,

The post coach comes rarely to the elves' Forest, but it came today. I am still with the greenies. The trading has been disappointing. They have not so much as showed me an Agulen no matter what I bring out to tempt them. Their chief trader, Slannen, knows little about bargaining. He gave me three vases in exchange for a gnomish copper stewpot, and the same for a simple wooden flute.

Below were three pages of trades and sales. He closed with his intentions.

I am making for Uaaxee's farm. You may remember Uaaxee, the giantess who entrusted her turnip harvest to me last year. On October 15, she will marry off her daughter and I shall be there. I should like to see a giant's wedding. The ritual is said to be peculiar. Moreover, several fairies are likely to be present. They say hardly a wedding or birth takes place without at least one in attendance. If I can persuade a few to reveal themselves, I may be able to pick up some fairy-made trifles.

I swallowed. My mouth had gone dry. Mandy had never told me that fairies liked to go to weddings and births. But she and Lucinda had both been present when I was born.

Perhaps Lucinda would go to the giants. It was the first time I'd ever known a definite place where she might be—where I might be too, if I could get there. She might even be in a generous frame of mind, especially if she had just cast a well-meant, horrible spell. Perhaps she'd be so pleased that she'd release me from mine if I begged her to.

I hadn't promised Father I would stay at finishing school, only that I would go. I could leave whenever I wanted. And by leaving, I'd never have to take another order from Hattie. Areida would still think I was her friend. And if I succeeded with Lucinda, I still could be.

How late was it? How much of the night was left for travel? I stood up, then sat down again. How far was Uaaxee's farm? The wedding was less than two weeks off. Could I get there in time?

Frantically, I riffled the pages of my book, hoping to be vouchsafed a map. There. But it was the same one I'd looked at in the carriage on the way to finishing school—of Frell, and no use to me now.

No matter. I'd get directions somehow.

In five minutes, my carpetbag was packed with a few essentials: Tonic, my magic book, my dictionary, a shawl, and little else. After a long look at Areida's sleeping form, I left.

I paused before the door to the Daisy Room, then went in. With quiet steps, I approached Hattie's bed. She frowned in her sleep and mumbled. I understood only one word: "royal."

Her wig was askew. Neat-fingered as I had become,

I was able to lift it off without waking her. Now, what to do with it? If I threw it into the dying fire, the smell might wake someone. I could drape it over the head of the china cat that adorned the mantelpiece, but if Hattie woke early, she could rescue it before anyone saw.

So I took it with me, a trophy.

CHAPTER THIRTEEN

I slipped through the sleeping house as silently as a needle through lace. Outside, I waved farewell to the sleeping topiary.

As I walked, the sky lightened. On the edge of Jenn, I gave a baker the first sale of the day, two currant muffins and two loaves of traveler's bread in exchange for Hattie's wig, which he declared the finest he'd ever seen.

He'd never heard of Uaaxee but said there were several giant farms "up north."

"I hear they bake cookies as wide as my waist," he said.

He drew a map for me in flour on his pastry board. The road would fork after I left Jenn. The right-hand fork led back to Frell. The left fork was the one I wanted. My first landmark would be the elves' Forest. After the Forest I would come to another fork. The road to the left, *which I was not to take*, led to the Fens, where the ogres lived. The road on the right would take me to the giants. When the cows became as big as barns, I would be there.

It didn't seem far on the pastry board. My fingers could travel the distance in a trice. The baker thought the trip would take five or six days by coach.

"How long do you think it would take to walk?"

"Walking?" He started to laugh. "On foot? Alone? With ogres and bandits roaming the road?"

Beyond Jenn, I left the road, following it, but too far away to be seen from it. I didn't fear pursuit by Madame Edith, who would probably conceal my disappearance for as long as possible in hopes I might return. The baker's worries about ogres and bandits I thought exaggerated, since a solitary traveler would hardly be worthwhile prey. However, I was wary of strangers. With my curse, I had to be.

I wondered if I would meet Char on his way to the Fens. I liked thinking he might be near, but whether he was ahead of me or behind, or whether he had taken this route at all, I had no idea, and I wished my magic book had told me more.

The road was little trafficked, and I was too happy about my escape to feel much fear. I was free of orders. If I wanted to eat my breakfast under a maple tree and watch the day grow between its leaves, I could—and did. If I wanted to skip or hop or run and slide on dew-wet leaves, I could—and did. And when the mood took me, I whistled or recited poems that I made up on the spot.

I spent two glorious days this way, the best since before Mother had died. I saw deer and hares, and once, at twilight, I swear I saw a phoenix rise, trailing smoke.

On the third day, I began to despair about reaching the giants in time. I hadn't even come to the elves' Forest. If I had any chance of getting to the wedding, I should have passed the Forest on the second day, unless the baker had been mistaken about the distance from the

Forest to the giants. Perhaps they were much closer to each other than he thought.

On the fourth day, I finished my last bit of traveler's bread. The land changed to sandy fields and low scrub, and I began to despair about reaching the giants before the newlyweds celebrated their first anniversary.

On the fifth day, I knew I was doomed to wander in endless barrens till I died.

On the sixth day, there were more trees, but I was too dazed by hunger to realize their significance. I was searching the ground for the lacy flowers of the wild carrot when I caught a shift in the shadows ahead of me, a flash of motion among the tree trunks. A deer? A walking bush? There. I saw it again. An elf!

"Kummeck ims powd," I called. It meant "sun and rain," or "hello" in Elfian.

"Kummeck ims powd." An elf woman approached me hesitantly. Her robe was woven in a dappled pattern, the shadow of leaves on the forest floor. "Speak Elfian?"

"Yun gar." ("A little.") I tried to smile at her, but her expression was so solemn I couldn't.

"Aff ench poel?" she asked.

"Dok ench Ella, jort hux Sir Peter hux Frell." I wondered if she knew Father.

"Sir Peter. Wattill len." Her tone was dismissive. She stepped closer and stared at me.

I met her gaze and hoped I didn't seem "wattill" ("sly") too.

Her eyes poured into me. I was sure she knew every one of my unkind thoughts, knew about the theft of Hattie's wig, knew each time I'd made my finishing school mistresses uncomfortable, and knew I hadn't had a bath since I'd left Jenn.

"Mund len." She smiled and took my hand. Her fingers felt waxy, like a leaf. "Not like father."

She led me to Slannen, the elves' chief trader, who spoke Kyrrian fluently. He was the one Father had mentioned in his letter.

He confirmed that the baker's map was accurate. I didn't say anything, but my face must have shown how bitter my disappointment was.

"You will join your father at the giant's farm?" he asked.

I nodded. "But I'm not hurrying to him," I blurted, then stopped.

"You seek something else from the giants?" His amber eyes searched my face.

"Someone I must find. I must find her."

Slannen patted my arm. "Elves will help. In the morning you will see. But you must spend the night as our guest." He smiled, showing pale-green teeth.

I smiled back, reassured—although one wouldn't expect green teeth to be reassuring.

The elves were the same height as humans. With their mossy hair and green skin tinged with orange for the coming autumn, they were no more frightening than a pumpkin vine.

"And now, please join us for our evening meal."

We sat at a table with twelve elves, who knew only a little Kyrrian. But with my bit of Elfian and gestures and laughter, we cobbled together a language understood by all.

Their supper was more drink than meal. The appetizer was lemon parsnip soup, followed by turtle barley soup (the main course), succeeded by a soup of chopped raw green vegetables (the salad course). Dessert was a fruit soup.

It was all delicious, even though my jaw wished for something to chew on. When we finished eating, Slannen said that elves liked to sleep soon after nightfall. He led me to my sleeping place.

We passed the elves' nursery, where clusters of small hammocks hung from trees like bunches of grapes. Two adult elves, one with a flute and one singing, threaded their way through, the singer occasionally rocking a group of hammocks gently.

When we reached the oak from which my hammock hung, I asked for a lantern to read by.

"What book is better than sleep when the sun goes down?" Slannen asked, calling for a light.

I had been afraid to show Mandy's present to anyone since Hattie had taken Mother's necklace. But now I produced it from my carpetbag.

Slannen opened it. "The Shoemaker and the Elves" returned as the first story. He roared with laughter. "We're so tiny in here! The elves can fit inside a shoe!"

He looked through the rest of the book, admiring the illustrations and reading parts of different stories. Then he turned back to "The Shoemaker and the Elves," but it was gone. In its place was a story about a walrus and a camel.

"Fairy made!" he cried. "This is precious. It must give you much comfort." He returned it to me. "Do not read too late. You have a long journey tomorrow."

After two stories, I blew out my light. The night was clear. My ceiling was sky and an eyelash of a moon. By shifting from side to side, I made my hammock swing me into sleep.

In the morning, Slannen asked me to show my book to the other elves. To them, it was written in Elfian. They were enchanted and might have read all day, except that Slannen stopped them.

"You have given us much pleasure," he said. "And now we'd like to show you something wonderful too."

He lifted several packages onto the table he used to display goods for trading. Then he began to remove their oak leaf wrappings.

"Are these by Agulen?" I asked when a bit of pottery emerged.

"You've heard of him," Slannen said, sounding pleased. "Yes, he made them."

A nut dish was unwrapped first. Modeled in the shape of a centaur, it rested on the table, but was in motion nonetheless. More than in motion—the centaur *was* motion. His head thrust into the wind; his arms hugged his form; his mane and tail streamed back; and, without moving—such was Agulen's skill—his legs beat the ground.

Next came a dragon-shaped coal scuttle that glowed gold and orange. Somehow, the air shimmered around its foot-long flame. Its ruby eyes were windows to an interior furnace. I was afraid to touch the beast for fear of being scorched.

But my favorite was a stirrup cup molded in the shape of a wolf's head and shoulders, with the head lifted and the mouth pulled into an O for a long howl. The ridges in the pottery for his fur were so fine that each hair was defined. I felt the tension in his shoulders where the cup ended, and I imagined the rest of him, sitting, but erect, with excitement running through him from his big paws to the end of his plumy tail.

I loved his howl, which I could both hear and feel: long and plaintive, woebegone and heartsore, filled with yearning for what used to be and for what would never come again.

"He's beautiful. They're all beautiful. They don't look as though someone made them. They look born."

Slannen began to wrap the pieces up again. I hated to let them go.

"Wrap this one last, please." I touched the wolf's nose.

When he finished, Slannen handed the package with the wolf to me. "It's for you."

Father had made clear that an Agulen was worth a great deal. "I can't accept such a valuable gift," I said in my best Manners Mistress manner. But my hands closed around it.

"You have," Slannen said, smiling. "We like to give our best pieces away sometimes, when we find people who love them."

"Thank you."

"Don't cry." Slannen gave me a green handkerchief. He looked at me consideringly. "Sir Peter is a witty man and a shrewd trader, but if he had admired our things as you do, we would have been gladder to let him have them."

"But he told me that you are the best potters."

"He should have told us. 'How can I exchange this

gnomish copper stewpot for two such paltry vases?' he'd say. 'The workmanship doesn't compare,' he'd say."

And Father had thought Slannen a poor trader!

My gift was packed on a fat pony along with enough food to last until I reached my destination—more elvish generosity (although the pony was a loan).

"Vib ol pess waddo," Slannen said in parting. ("Stay in the shade.") "With any luck you will reach the giants in three or four days."

But I had no luck.

CHAPTER FOURTEEN

The morning after I left the elves, an ogre woke me by poking me with a stick. "Wake up, Breakfast. How do you like to be cooked? Bloody? Medium? Or done to a crisp?"

Eight ogres surrounded me.

"It will only hurt for a minute." My ogre (the one who woke me) stroked my cheek. "I'm a fast eater."

I looked at the others, searching vainly for a sympathetic face. Not far off, I saw my saddlebags, next to a pile of bones. Whose bones? I hated to think. Then I realized. The elves' pony. I swallowed convulsively. My stomach heaved and I threw up.

When I was done, my ogre spat at me. His spittle burned my cheek. I wiped it off with my hand, and my hand burned too.

"forns uiv eMMong FFnOO ehf nushOOn," he growled. ("It will taste sour for hours.") I was an it—I had studied sufficient Ogrese to understand almost everything.

One of the women spoke. I think she was a woman because there was less hair on her face and she was shorter than my ogre, and I think he was a man. She called my ogre SEEf and asked him if he thought he was going to eat it all by himself. He answered that he'd found it and caught it, so it belonged to him. Anyway, he added, if he shared, there wouldn't be enough to go around. And besides, he'd allowed everyone to eat the pony.

Her answer was that the pony had been last night, that they were hungry again, that he always had a hundred reasons not to share, and that he didn't care if the whole tribe starved so long as he got his special treat.

He lunged at her and she lunged at him. In a moment, they were rolling on the ground, with everyone watching.

Except me. I looked for a place to hide. Not far from where I stood was a low tree still covered with leaves. If I could get there and climb it, maybe they wouldn't think to look up when they searched for me.

I edged sideways. The combatants were pulling each other's hair and biting and yelling. I was halfway to the tree.

"It's escaping, SEEf!" one of the ogres yelled.

The brawl ended immediately.

"Stop!" SEEf commanded in Kyrrian.

I took a few more steps and almost reached the tree, but the curse wouldn't let me go farther.

SEEf dusted himself off, although there was no visible difference between dusty and dusted. "I told you how obedient it is," he said in Ogrese. "No need to be persuasive with this one. It'd cook itself if we told it to."

He was right. If they wanted to fry me, I'd step right into the pan. I stood where I was and pretended I had no idea what they were saying.

After further bickering, they decided to take me with

them, hoping to capture additional people or animals on the road to eat along with me. Side dishes, I supposed.

I was allowed to take my saddlebags and my carpetbag. SEEf wanted to know if there was food in them, and there was great excitement when I said yes. But when they opened the elves' flasks, they spat in disgust.

"lahlFFOOn! ruJJ!" ("Vegetables! Fish!") The ogres pronounced the words as though they were poisonous.

SEEf scratched his head. "I wonder how it can eat those things and still taste good," he said.

"Maybe it doesn't taste good. We haven't eaten it yet." The speaker was the ogre who had warned of my escape. He was younger than the others, approximately my own age.

We set out on the road, moving almost as quickly as my pony had. I had to ride on their shoulders, holding their oily hair. We were traveling away from Uaaxee's farm, back the way I'd come. I assumed the ogres meant to go to the fork in the road and proceed to their Fens. It made no difference. What did it matter if I were devoured ten miles from my destination or forty?

No one was on the road, and the hills through which we marched were empty of habitation. The ogres began to grumble.

"It gets heavier every mile."

"Perhaps it brings bad luck."

"We should eat it tonight and find more tomorrow."

They watched me enviously while I drank the elves' supper. I was surprised I could eat, but I was ravenous. I offered to share with them, but my only answer was a collective shudder.

"You might enjoy it," I said. "Perhaps you'd find that you prefer broccoli to flesh and legumes to legs."

The last suggestion made them laugh.

The youngest ogre told SEEf in Ogrese, "Maybe we should get to know our meals better. This one makes jokes."

"Don't make a pet out of it," SEEf warned.

After dinner the young ogre sat next to me. "You mustn't be frightened," he said.

No?

"My name is NiSSh. What's yours?"

I told him.

"My father's name is SEEf. He could convince you that we won't harm you. I'm not as good at convincing people yet. But we hate for people to be upset." He touched my arm sympathetically.

I felt calmer. I couldn't help it. His voice was so soothing.

"You must be tired, after such a terrible day."

I yawned.

"Why don't you stretch out right here? I'll make sure nothing harms you while you sleep."

Wasn't he going to bind me? A bubble of hope swelled in my mind.

"But don't run away."

The bubble burst.

In the middle of the night I awoke. SEEf slept closest to me, making gurgling noises and grinding his teeth.

Ogres are sound sleepers. I stood and picked my way over them, which was difficult because they slept almost on top of one another. I bumped the leg of one, and he or she kicked at me but slept on. Beyond the heap of their bodies, I found my saddlebags.

I tried to leave, but as soon as I crept more than a few yards beyond the pile of ogres, my complaints started: thudding heart, tight chest, spinning head. A few feet more, and I was on my knees, crawling in circles. I crept back to the farthest spot the curse let me feel comfortable.

The ogres wouldn't wait much longer to kill me. I had to break the spell now.

"The spell is broken," I announced aloud, but softly. "I need not obey NiSSh. I will escape."

But in a moment I was on my knees again, helpless and sobbing.

I tried again. Mimicking the ogres, I made my voice as persuasive as I could. "What is a spell?" I asked myself. "Only words. I can walk away from these ogres. I can do it. No magic can stop me."

I stood and took confident steps. I was moving quickly, fearlessly. The spell was broken!

Then I saw SEEf almost at my feet. I had gone the wrong way.

I bit back a scream of rage. I was going to die soon, and I would never have found Lucinda, would never have lived uncursed.

I returned to the end of my invisible tether and battled my despair. My voice had been persuasive; might not persuasion have other uses? Could I mimic the ogres? Could I speak with their persuasive power?

For a while my voice sounded too harsh. It needed honey for sweetness and oil for smoothness. I imagined swallowing a mixture of the two and coating my throat with them.

"SSyng lahlFFOOn, haZZ liMMOOn. lahlFFOOn eFFuth wAAth psySSahbuSS." It meant "One should eat vegetables, not humans, because vegetables taste more delicious." It sounded persuasive to me. I was convinced.

I practiced for hours and fell asleep practicing.

And woke up to NiSSh, practicing on me. "Wake up, dearie. You were wise not to leave us during the night. These lands are dangerous. An elf might have gotten you."

The image of a fierce, spear-carrying elf came to me.

"Let's eat it now," said a female ogre. "You can't have all of it, SEEf. We'll get more food soon."

"All right, if I get a leg." He held my shoulders.

She nodded. "I'll be content with an arm if I can have an ear too."

In a moment all my parts were claimed. NiSSh wanted to keep me alive awhile longer, but he gave in when he was allowed to have my neck.

"The best part," he said, coming close and patting it.

SEEf said, "I want to be the one to kill it." He jerked me away from NiSSh.

"You're . . ." I began in Ogrese. It came out as a squeak.

SEEf bared his teeth. The points glistened. Saliva dripped from his lips.

I tried again. "You're not really hungry. You're full." My voice was raspy. More honey! More oil!

The ogres stared, as surprised as if a rock had spoken.

"I knew it was smart." NiSSh sounded proud of me.

"Too bad we're hungry." SEEf crouched. "It would have made a good pet." He held my leg, his portion, and lowered his head, his teeth inches from my thigh.

Honey and oil! "How can you eat me? You're too full to eat—all of you are. Your bellies are as heavy as sacks of melons."

SEEf stopped.

I went on. "You just had a wonderful meal of eight fat ladies. If you eat me too, you'll get sick. You want to go back to sleep, to sleep off your big meal."

SEEf let me go. I stepped away from him.

"You feel tired. The ground is so soft, so comfortable," I said.

NiSSh rubbed his eyes and stretched.

I continued, soothingly. "It's much too early to be awake. The day has barely begun, and it will be a lovely, lazy, sleepy day."

SEEf sat. His head rolled onto his chest.

"You can sleep and have delicious dreams. While you're sleeping, I'll find you another enormous meal, of piglets and people and elves and elephants and horses and . . ."

"No hornets," NiSSh muttered from a dream.

Sleep had claimed them. They had returned to their heap of the night, again grunting and snoring and groaning.

I almost laughed and broke the spell. Who was giving orders now?

CHAPTER FIFTEEN

I sobered quickly. What was I going to do with them? How could I arrive at Uaaxee's farm with eight ogres in tow?

My situation hadn't improved significantly. I was still alive, but not for long. I would have to sleep eventually. Then they'd awaken and remember their true hunger.

A twig snapped behind me. I turned and saw a vision: six knights carrying rope strode toward me, led by a tall young man.

Visions don't snap twigs. And the young man was Char!

He saluted me, but his eyes were on the ogres. Uncoiling a length of rope, he knelt over SEEf and began to bind his ankles.

The ogres slept soundly, but they were not unconscious. As soon as he felt the cord tighten, SEEf woke with a roar, which shrank to a purr when he saw Char.

"What an honor, your Highness. But why do you bind an ally?" He reached down and loosened the rope.

That was proper. Char shouldn't have been fettering his friend.

But Char pushed SEEf's hands aside and tightened the rope again. How could he be so cruel?

The knights had begun to bind the other ogres, who were also stirring.

SEEf tried again. "Prince, I would sacrifice my life for you, and you treat me so rudely."

Still, Char paid no attention. I watched stupidly while SEEf's feet lashed out. Char reeled back, losing his grip on the rope. SEEf rose and kicked the tether away.

The knights hadn't made much progress with their binding either. Everywhere, they were doing battle. An ogre knelt over one fallen knight, about to sink teeth into his shoulder. The knight twisted away, gaining a few seconds, but the ogre was turning toward him.

Char regained his feet and drew his sword. He and SEEf faced each other warily. Char spoke to me, his voice oddly loud.

"Can you tame them again, Ella? If not, run and save yourself."

The question cleared my wits.

"SEEf, NiSSh, ogre friends," I called in Ogrese. "Why do you wish to destroy your benefactors? They have food for you, but they cannot give it to you until you do what they want."

The ogres stopped clawing and biting and pounding and lunging and kicking and looked at me trustfully.

"Would you like to know what the food is?" I asked.

"Please," SEEf said.

"The treat they have for you is a dozen baby giants only six months old."

They all smiled beatifically.

"But these friends can't bring the feast unless you let them tie and gag you. When they bring out the infants, they'll remove your bindings. So seat yourselves and hold out your arms and legs. They will be gentle."

Only NiSSh remained standing, looking dazed.

"Sit," SEEf commanded.

NiSSh sat. The tying and gagging was completed quickly. Then the ogres were bound together, treatment that they endured cheerfully.

"Ella . . ." Char swept a deep bow. He'd grown taller. "How did you tame the ogres?" His voice was too loud again.

"I'm skilled at tongues, and—"

"I can't hear you. Oh, I forgot." He extracted something from his ears—beeswax.

"That's why the ogres' magic had no effect on you."

"Once we sight ogres, we always put the wax in. The danger is being caught unawares."

Char said that one of the knights, acting as a scout, had seen me. "He reported that a band of ogres was about to eat a maiden when she talked them to sleep. How did you do it?"

"I told them about finishing school, and they began to snore."

"Truly?" Char stared at me, then laughed.

It was delightful to make him laugh. He was always so surprised.

"How did you really do it?" he persisted.

"I spoke to them in Ogrese, and I imitated their oily way of talking. I didn't know if I would succeed. They had already parceled me up. I knew which one was going to eat every bit of me. SEEf—that one—wanted my leg."

Char moved his own right leg. "How did they come upon you?"

I told him I had run away from finishing school. "They caught me when I left the elves. They ate the pony the elves gave me." I shuddered.

"Was finishing school so wearisome that you had to run away?" he asked.

"Very wearisome, and see what it's done to me. I can no longer break a set of dishes by accident. Now I can balance all of them on my head and stroll through Frell without dropping a single one. I have many accomplishments."

"Are you proud of them?" He was alarmed.

I nodded solemnly. I wanted to make him laugh again. "Would you like to know more?"

He shrugged, disliking the topic.

I went on anyway. "To begin with, I could teach these boorish ogres how to eat properly." I seated myself on a large rock. "Observe." I plucked an imaginary napkin out of the air, shook it twice, and placed it on my lap.

"Very ladylike," Char said politely.

"I shake the napkin twice. That's important."

"Why?"

"Mice."

Char smiled. "There are no mice in our court napkins. You are thinking of spiders."

"The prince contradicts a lady!" I picked up an imaginary fork and began to saw at imaginary food.

"Your meat is tough. You have a low regard for our cooks."

"Not at all. It should be tough. Don't you know why?"

"Tell me."

"It is mutton. Am I not using a mutton fork? Our Manners Mistress will believe you're an impostor if you don't recognize a mutton fork when . . ."

"When I don't see one." He was laughing.

"It could only be a mutton fork!"

"How so?"

"See how my fingers are bunched together at the top of the stem." I reached up and caught Char's hand. It was square and large.

I extended my index finger. "My finger is the fork. You grasp it so." I arranged his fingers around mine. His grip was firm. "That's the only correct way to hold a mutton fork. A trout fork is managed differently." I turned his hand over to demonstrate. Angry red welts ran across his palm. "The rope burned you!"

He pulled his hand away. "It's nothing. One of the knights is a healer. What else did your Manners Mistress teach you?"

I wanted to examine the burn more closely, but I continued. "Manners Mistress knew your father's opinion about everything. She said he would exile any subject who ate blancmange from a soup bowl. As a result of her instruction, I can never make such a mistake."

"Does my father have a special spoon for raspberries and one for blueberries?"

"Certainly."

"Why wasn't I informed?"

"You should hire Manners Mistress. She would die of delight to serve a prince."

I went on to describe all our mistresses. "Writing Mistress was the only one who taught anything worth knowing," I concluded, "although it *is* helpful to know the proper way to behave, so one can decide whether or not to be proper."

On the word "proper," Char started. "I should have introduced you long ago to my knights." He called to them. "Friends—John, Aubrey, Bertram, Percival, Martin, Stephan—meet our ogre tamer. She's the lass I told you about, the one who speaks Gnomic."

He had told them about me! I curtsied.

"We wondered when you would remember your manners," the one named Stephan said.

SEEf made a garbled noise through his gag. For a moment I had forgotten him. Char went to the ogres, and I followed.

"So much as you are our friends, so much are we your friends," he said. "But we won't kill you unless you force us to."

For an instant, SEEf looked dumbstruck. Then he began to struggle violently against his bonds. The other ogres did likewise, and shrieked through their gags as well.

The ropes held, and they quieted slowly.

SEEf glared at me with such rage and hate that I fell back a step. I held his gaze, however.

"You are never going to eat me," I told him in Ogrese. "I am not an 'it.' And I'm not your dinner. And how do you like being tricked into doing what you don't want to do?"

Telling them felt wonderful. I smiled at Char. For some reason, he blushed.

While Char and I addressed the ogres, the knights were busy setting out lunch for all of us. When we were seated, we delayed our first bite until Char began to eat.

It was so natural to him I doubted he noticed. Over traveler's bread, cheese, dried meats, and sweet cider, he told me about his mission to help King Jerrold.

"The king will be glad to see this lot. Eight ogres and no injury to us." Sir Stephan nodded at the ogres, who were struggling anew at the sight of our meal.

"He'll be interested to learn that humans can use their magic against them," Char said. "At least Ella can."

"Whenever he finds out." Sir Bertram frowned. "How will we convey them to King Jerrold?"

"No need for your melancholy, Sir Bert," Sir John said. "With this maid's help, we just caught eight ogres. Six knights never did that before."

"We'll think of something," Char said.

"They'll have to be fed." Sir Bertram reached for the bread.

"And you're the best hunter we have, Sir Bert," Char said, and the knight's expression lightened.

"Ogres can move quickly," Sir Martin said. "It shouldn't take too long to reach the king."

"I've been told they can outrun a horse," Sir Stephan added. "A centaur too. Even a hart."

While Char and the knights discussed ogre transport, I thought about the wedding and despaired of getting there in time. It was three days from now, and I was even farther from the giants than I had been when the ogres had captured me. If I walked, I would arrive weeks late. And then I remembered NiSSh's order not to run away. I could not leave anyway.

Sir Bertram's gloomy voice penetrated my thoughts. "We'll have to drag them. And how can we do that?"

"The young lady can tell them to go wherever we

say," Sir Aubrey said. "She can come with us and keep them biddable."

"Let the prince tell us what to do," Sir Stephan said. "He knows."

Char spoke confidently. "You, Stephan, will escort the Lady Ella to her destination, wherever that is. Martin and Percival will ride to my father for assistance. Sir Bert, Aubrey, John, and I shall take turns hunting and guarding the ogres. We'll put the wax back in our ears when we are within earshot of them in case their gags slip."

"I'd rather stay with you, lad," Sir Martin said.

"You and Percival are our best scouts. We'll depend on you to get through quickly."

Sir Martin nodded.

"The maiden will be safe with me," Sir Stephan vowed. "I'll—"

"Unless he talks her to death," Sir Aubrey interrupted. "You don't know him, lady. His speech stops only when the stars shine green in a yellow sky."

"He'll be a better companion than ogres," Char said. "But, Ella, why didn't you go back to Frell when you left finishing school?"

"My father is trading at a giant's farm, where a wedding will take place soon. He wrote that giants' weddings are interesting. I thought I'd join him there."

Char marveled. "You put yourself in such danger in order to see a wedding?"

He thought me a fool.

Sir Bertram spoke. "It's fortunate that all the maidens in Kyrria do not decide to travel by themselves. We have work enough without having to rescue them."

"If all the maids in Kyrria could tame ogres," Char said, "we would have much less to do."

Perhaps not such a fool, after all.

After lunch Sir Stephan mounted his horse, and Char lifted me behind him. As soon as he did, my curse-caused complaints began. In a moment I was going to fall off the horse. The curse wasn't going to let me abandon the ogres.

"I don't like to leave you in danger," I said, starting to dismount.

"Go with Sir Stephan," said Char. "We won't come to harm."

It was an order. I could go. My symptoms stopped.

Char caught the horse's bridle. "Will you soon be in Frell again?"

"If Father doesn't send me back to finishing school, and if he doesn't want me to travel with him." Why did he want to know? Did he want me to be? "Why do you ask?"

He didn't answer directly. "I should be back shortly. These maneuvers never last long." He spoke as though he'd been on thousands.

"Perhaps I'll see you soon then, and you can tell me about the other ogres you catch."

"Perhaps you can teach me how to tame an ogre."

"ahthOOn SSyng!" I said. "That's farewell."

"It sounds evil."

"It is," I answered, and we parted.

CHAPTER SIXTEEN

Sir Stephan was indeed talkative. He had a small manor in Frell, a wife, four daughters, and two hounds. The hounds were the joy of his life. "Smarter than pigs, cats, and dragons all rolled together," he said. As we rode, he recounted tale after tale of their bravery and cleverness.

"When do you think we'll reach the giants?" I asked when he stopped for breath.

"Three days, I should think."

The day of the wedding! And we might arrive after it ended.

"Can we go any faster? I don't need much sleep."

"Maybe you don't, and I'm eager to get back to those ogres. But the horse needs his rest. We'll go as fast as he'll take us."

I kicked the horse, hoping to spur him on and hoping Sir Stephan wouldn't notice. Sir Stephan didn't, and the horse didn't either.

Sir Stephan began a tale about exhausted horses and a charge against a dragon. When he finished, I hastily changed the subject.

"Do you like serving under the prince?"

"Some might not fancy answering to a youngster," he said, "but I'm a toiling knight."

"What's that?"

"Not so noble I can't curry my own horse, nor so greedy I have no time to serve my king."

"Is Char a 'toiling prince'?"

"That's a good description of him, little lady. I never saw a lad, page or prince, so eager to learn to do a thing right."

According to Sir Stephan, Char was almost as wonderful as the hounds. He wasn't only eager to learn, he did learn, and quickly. He was kind. They had departed Frell late because of his kindness. The cart of a fruit-and-vegetable seller had overturned in the road ahead of them.

"When the seller began screeching that everyone would trample his precious tomatoes and melons and lettuces, Char had us right the cart; then he spent the better part of an hour on his hands and knees, rescuing vegetables."

"As he rescued me."

"You're a long mile prettier than a grape or a squash, and you needed a long mile less rescuing. I never caught an ogre so neatly before."

I turned the conversation away from me and back to Char.

"He's smart and he's steady, the prince is," Sir Stephan continued. "Too steady, maybe. Too serious, maybe. He laughs when there's something to laugh at, but he doesn't play enough. He's been with the king's councillors too much." Sir Stephan was quiet for a rare moment. "He laughed more in a morning with you than in two weeks with us. He should frolic with the young folks more, but they're on their best behavior with a prince." He turned his head. "Except for you, little lady."

I was alarmed. "Did I behave badly?"

"You acted natural. Not like a courtier."

Manners Mistress would consider me an utter failure. I smiled.

We spent our nights at inns. The first night I retired to my room soon after dinner. I set my Agulen wolf on the table next to my bed so he could protect my sleep. Then I opened my magic book.

On the verso was a letter from Hattie to her mother. On the recto, one to the same lady from Olive. I read Hattie's first.

Dear Mama,

Is not my penmanship much improoved? I have been practicing my flurrishes. The words may be harder to read, and Writing Mistress dispares of my spelling, but when you stand away from the page, is the result not charming?

Sir Peter's daughter has vanished. Madame Edith says she was called away in the night. However, I suspect that Madame Edith is lying and that Ella has run off. There was always something devious and deceetful about her, although her father is such a charming, rich man.

My new tresses are divine, and I emmerged among the other girls again two days ago when they arrived. I suspect my locks may have vanished with Ella. A hartless prank to play on me, who always treated her with kindness. But I still hope she has come to no harm and has not been eaten by ogres or captured by bandits or caught fire or fallen into bad company, as I often imagine.

The rest of the letter recounted the compliments Hattie had received on a new gown. She ended with a farewell and the largest flourish of all—*Hattie*.

The recto:

Deer Muther,

I hav ben feeling poarly all week. I hav hedakes espeshly wen I reed. You allways say to much reeding is bad for the iyes but Writting Mistress wont lissen. She called me littel moar than an iddiot and sed ther will be no hop for me when I am gron if I dont lern to reed better.

Hattie says Ella was bad to leeve but I think she was bad not to tak me to.

Ella did everything Hattie toled her to. I wish peepul did wat I want. Its not fare.

Yoar mizrubbel dawter,
Olive

The whole page was full of blots and cross-outs. Each letter was formed with a wobbly hand, as though the writer didn't know how to hold a pen. Poar Olive!

Her letter was followed by a sad tale about the genie in Aladdin's lamp. He had been forced by Aladdin's false uncle, the magician, to take up residence in the lamp and had been given power to grant everyone's wishes but his own. Before he was captured, he had been in love with a goose girl. The genie spent his years in the lamp longing for her and wondering whether she'd married someone else, whether she'd grown old, whether she'd died.

I closed the book, weeping a little. I wasn't confined to a lamp, but I too was not free.

ঙ

The size of things began to grow shortly after we started out on the third morning. In the past, objects far away had always appeared smaller than objects close by. But now, the old rule stood on its head. The trees near us were dwarfed by the trees in the distance ahead. At ten o'clock, I saw a pumpkin as wide as I was tall. At eleven, we passed one as big as a carriage.

At noon, we saw a giant. He was building a stone wall out of boulders. It was already twice my height, and I shuddered to think of the livestock it would pen.

When the giant saw us, he trumpeted his pleasure. "Oooayaagik (*honk*)!" he called, dropping a rock and thundering toward us, his mouth open wide in a huge smile of welcome.

Our horse reared in fright, and I struggled to keep my seat, till the giant reached down and touched the beast gently on his muzzle. He quieted instantly, and even nuzzled against the giant's thigh.

"Aaaope! Aiiiee uuu koobee (*screech*) ooob payiipe aau," I said. It meant "hello" in Abdegi. "We've come to attend the wedding of Uaaxee's daughter," I added in Kyrrian. "But are we too late?"

"You're just in time. I'll lead you there."

The farm was two hours away. Koopooduk, the giant, strolled next to our horse.

"Is Uaaxee expecting you?" he asked.

"No," I answered. "Will she mind?"

"Mind? She won't be able to thank you enough for coming. Giants love strangers." He paused. "And friends too. Lots of friends and strangers will be there."

We traveled in silence for a while, with Koopooduk smiling down at us.

"Are you tired? Hungry?" he asked presently.

"We're fine," Sir Stephan said, although I was starving.

"Everyone is polite, except giants. We say when we're hungry. Never mind. There's lots to eat at a giant's farm."

Uaaxee's house was visible an hour before we reached it.

"That's her house," Koopooduk announced, pointing. "It's nice, isn't it?"

"Enormously nice. Hugely nice," Sir Stephan said. "Don't you think so, lass?"

I nodded. My heart began to pound so hard I thought it would catapult me backward off the horse. Soon I might find Lucinda. Soon I might be free.

CHAPTER SEVENTEEN

I tightened my grip on Sir Stephan's waist.

"Do you think to be my corset?" he complained.

As we approached, Uaaxee opened the door to look for new guests. We were still a distance from the house, so I was able to see her whole. Close up, giants were whatever part was nearest—a skirt, a bodice, a trouser leg, or a face.

She was three times as tall as a grown human, but no wider. Everything about her was long and narrow: head, torso, arms, legs. However, when she saw us, the long oval of her face changed. She smiled so broadly that her cheeks became peach round, and her eyes behind her spectacles became slits of delight.

"Aiiiee koobee (*screech*) deegu (*whistle*)!" She lifted Sir Stephan off the horse and then saw me. "Two people! Oooayaagik (*honk*) to both of you! Welcome! The wedding will be in a little while. Udabee!" she called to her daughter, the bride. "Look who's here."

The daughter, surrounded by friends, waved to us.

"I can't stay, madam. I just brought this young lady to find her father."

"Her father?"

"Sir Peter of Frell," I said.

Uaaxee beamed. "So this is his daughter! He never

said a word." She turned toward the house. "Where is he? I'll find him. He'll be so glad you're here."

"Please don't," I said quickly. "I want to surprise him."

"Surprise! I love surprises. I won't tell."

Sir Stephan mounted his horse. "I must go. Good-bye, Ella, madam."

"But how can you leave the party? You didn't even come in!"

Sir Stephan looked up at Uaaxee's long face, even longer in distress.

"Madam, it grieves me to go," he said. "Only a matter of the utmost urgency could take me away." He winked at me. "Please don't be sad. I'll only be able to comfort myself if I believe you are happy."

Uaaxee smiled through tears. "At least let me give you food for your journey." She hurried into the house, calling behind her, "I'll only be a moment."

"Toiling knights are also diplomats," I said.

"When we have to be. I'll tell the prince I left you in large, good hands."

Uaaxee returned with a hamper from which protruded a chicken wing as big as a turkey. Sir Stephan galloped off and Uaaxee hurried away, diverted by new guests.

I entered the house and joined the throng. I could see nothing except the people (or parts of them) nearest me: a group of gnomes arguing about mining techniques, and the skirts of two giantesses. How would I manage to find one human-sized fairy? The only clue would be her tiny feet, and they would be hidden by her skirts.

Giants crowded around a table so tall that I could

walk beneath it without bumping my head. On the other side, I came to a stool loaded with food for the small people. While I searched, I might as well eat. I filled my plate (a saucer as big as a platter) with a slice of potato, three foot-long string beans, and a balloon-sized cheese puff.

It was impossible to eat this food and walk. With a napkin draped over my arm and trailing on the floor, I made my way to one of the giant pillows that lined the walls of the dining hall—couches for humans, elves, and gnomes. I would watch the crowd while I dined.

The silverware was too big. I looked around to see how others were managing. Some struggled with knives and forks the size of axes and shovels, some stared at their meal in perplexity. And some dug in with bare hands.

The string beans and potato slice were easy. I held them in both hands and ate. Not so the cheese puff. It oozed when I bit in, and half my face was covered with cheese.

As I cleaned myself, a gong rang out. The deep, booming sound resonated in my chest. The wedding would begin soon.

I followed the crowd as it trooped outdoors. Unconfined by walls, it thinned, and I was able to take in more of the guests at a glance. And there was Father, only a few yards ahead of me, also searching. I stood still and allowed several giants to separate us. Then I hurried to stay close behind them. In their midst I slipped past Father.

After half an hour we reached a cleared field where stands had been erected for giants and smaller peoples. A few humans had arrived and had seated themselves. I slipped behind a tall man, where I would be well concealed. I was close to the aisle and in a good position to scrutinize the feet of new arrivals. The ladies had to lift their skirts as they climbed. At each step up a boot appeared or a slipper peeped out. I counted them off.

Ordinary foot. Ordinary. Large. Quite large.

The benches were almost full. Father arrived and seated himself far from me.

Ordinary foot. Small, but not small enough. Ordinary. Ordinary. Ordinary. Very tiny! Very tiny!

The two lady fairies, accompanied by a gentleman (who was surely a fairy too), squeezed into the row only two below mine. The gentleman was stoop shouldered and one of the ladies was fat. But the other satisfied every cherished idea of a fairy: tall and graceful, with huge eyes, skin as unblemished as satin, lips as red as pomegranate seeds, and cheeks the color of early sunset.

The stands were too crowded; I couldn't approach them, but I'd watch to make sure they didn't leave.

The wedding began.

The bride and groom came into the field holding hands. She carried a sack, and he carried a hoe. Each wore trousers and a white smock.

At the sight of them, a roar rose from the giants' stands. Giants screeched, moaned, grunted, and hummed that the bride was beautiful, the groom was handsome, they would be healthy for long and forever, and this was the happiest day in anybody's memory.

Aside from enormous smiles, the couple ignored them and began to plant a row of corn. He prepared the ground, and she dropped in seeds from her sack and covered them with moist earth.

As they finished, clouds rolled in and a gentle rain fell, although the sky had been clear when the ceremony started. The giants spread their arms and tilted their heads to receive the drops.

I looked down at the fairies. The two plain ones were smiling, but the beautiful one was rapturous. She seemed to be singing, and tears rolled down her cheeks.

The giants pantomimed their lives together. They farmed and built a house and brought a series of older and older children from the audience into the imaginary home, and then more babies for grandchildren. It ended when they lay down in the grass to signify their deaths together.

Then they sprang up. Benches were overturned as giants poured onto the field to hug them and exclaim over the ceremony.

I stayed in my place, marveling. These giants were lucky to see their lives laid out so sweetly before them. Did the pantomime help? Did it stop ogres from eating you? Did it prevent droughts and floods? Did it keep you from dying before your children were grown?

Except for the beautiful fairy and a number of giants, everyone started back to the house, including Father. I stayed to watch the fairy, hoping—praying—that she would reveal herself to be Lucinda. She pushed her way to the newlyweds through a crowd of relatives and well-wishers.

In a few minutes the giants drew away from her. The bride and groom clutched each other. Both were crying. Uaaxee appeared to be pleading. She crouched before the fairy so that their faces were level, and her eyes never left the fairy.

The fairy stroked Uaaxee's arm sympathetically, but Uaaxee flinched at the touch. Finally the giants turned and walked slowly back to the house. The fairy watched them go, smiling blissfully.

This had to be Lucinda. There was every sign of it. She had probably bestowed a gift on the newlyweds that was as gladly received as mine had been.

"Lady . . ." I called, my heart pounding.

She didn't hear me. As I spoke, she vanished, without even a puff of smoke or a shimmer in the air to mark her departure. Now I knew for certain she was Lucinda, the only fairy in the world who would disappear in plain view.

"Fool!" I called myself. "Idiot!" I should have spoken to her the moment I suspected who she was. She could be in Ayortha by now, or soaring over an ocean.

I returned to the house and found that the giants had grown somber, although the small people were still merry. I wandered through the hall, munching on this and that, while watching out for Father. Where should I go next? How could I continue my quest?

The other fairies might still be here and might know where Lucinda had gone. Quickening my pace, I began to search, and in a few minutes I saw them, standing together and looking as sorrowful as the giants. When I had almost reached them, Lucinda materialized in their midst, still smiling.

I pretended to be utterly absorbed in the problem of cracking a gigantic walnut I had taken from the banquet stool.

"I won't waste my breath telling you how wrong it is to disappear and reappear as you do," the gentleman fairy told Lucinda. "I hope you don't plan to do it again in the middle of this crowd."

"No, Cyril. How could I leave the scene of my greatest triumph?" Her voice was musical. I smelled lilacs.

"What horror did you visit on this poor couple?" he asked.

"No horror, a gift!"

"What gift, then?" the other lady fairy asked.

"Ah, Claudia. I gave them companionship and felicitous union."

Cyril raised his eyebrows. "How did you accomplish that?"

"I gave them the gift of being together always. They can go nowhere without each other. Isn't it splendid?"

The walnut almost slipped from my hands.

"It's frightful," Cyril said.

"What's wrong with it?" Lucinda thrust her head forward defiantly.

"They'll hate each other within a month," Claudia answered.

Lucinda laughed, a pretty, tinkling sound. "No they won't. They'll love each other more than ever."

Cyril shook his head. "If they argue—and all loving couples argue—they'll never be alone to recollect themselves, to find ways to forgive each other."

"You know nothing about it. Not all couples argue, and these two won't. They're too much in love."

"Imagine he bites his nails, and she doesn't like it," Claudia said. "Or she rocks back and forth when she talks, and he doesn't like it—they will never have any respite from the quality they don't like. It will grow and grow until all he sees in her is rocking and all she sees in him is nail-biting."

"My gift has nothing to do with nails and rocking. It has to do with the heart, which loves to be near that which it loves."

I forgot my walnut and stared at the mad fairy.

"Visit again in a year," Cyril challenged. "You'll see what the heart loves."

"From now on all giants will elope," Claudia said, "rather than risk a wedding with you as a guest."

"I shall return! And I'll be right and they'll thank—What are you staring at? I mean you! Wench!" Lucinda whirled on me.

CHAPTER EIGHTEEN

She's probably another supplicant," Cyril said, "come to beg you to take away a gift you gave her at birth."

"Don't turn this one into a squirrel. I can't bear to watch it." Claudia grasped Lucinda's wrist. "You can't know squirrels lead 'charming, contented lives.' I'm sure she prefers to be a human maiden."

A squirrel! I had to keep her from making a squirrel of me.

"Abensa eke ubassu inouxi Akyrria," I said, wondering if she spoke Ayorthaian. I had just told her I didn't understand Kyrrian.

Lucinda's expression softened. "I'm sorry, my sweet," she answered in Ayorthaian. "I asked why you were staring at me."

"You're so beautiful." Let her think me simple.

"What a darling child! What's your name, dear?"

"Elle." This was Ella in Ayorthaian.

"Beauty isn't important, Elle. Only what's in your heart is important. Do you understand that?"

"Yes. I'm sorry I stared."

"No need to be sorry, sweet child. You did nothing wrong." Her smile was dazzling.

"Thank you, lady." I curtsied.

"You may call me Lucinda." She lifted her chin. "They would not have me say so"—she indicated Cyril and Claudia—"but I am a fairy."

"A fairy! That's why you're so beautiful."

"My friends—"

"Are shopkeepers," Cyril said firmly, also in Ayorthaian. "We sell shoes."

"For tiny feet." Lucinda laughed.

"For children," Claudia amended.

"Oh," I said. "I don't need shoes, but I need help, magical help. Can you help me, Lady Lucinda?"

"You don't need her help," Claudia said. "You should leave her while you still may."

"I'd be delighted to help you. You see, Claudia, they do need us. Tell me, Elle."

"I want more mettle, if you please, lady. Whatever anyone tells me to do, I do, whether I want to or not. I've always been this way, but I wish I weren't."

"The maiden is naturally obedient," Cyril said. "Isn't that one of your gifts? And she doesn't like it."

"I knew how sweet you were the moment I saw you. Obedience is a marvelous gift, Elle. Sometimes I give that gift to little babies. I certainly won't take it away from you. Be happy to be blessed with such a lovely quality."

"But . . ." I began, then stopped as Lucinda's order gripped me. My mood changed, and I smiled joyously. The curse had been turned into a blessing. "Thank you, lady! Thank you," I said, almost forgetting to speak Ayorthaian. I kissed her hand.

"There, there. You don't have to thank me. You only needed to see it in the proper light." She patted my head. "Now run along, Elle."

My first order in my new state. I was delighted to obey. I rushed off.

I knew I was happy only because I'd been ordered to be, but the happiness was absolute. I still understood why I had always hated Lucinda's gift. But I was glad nonetheless. I imagined future commands, awful ones, ones that would kill me, and I glowed at the idea of obeying them.

For the first time since Mother had died, I was free of fear. I would embrace whatever happened. I felt as light as a cloud.

I decided to find Father. If anyone would have commands for me, he would. I found him outside Uaaxee's house, climbing into his carriage. He turned when he heard my voice, and I received a shock. He was actually pleased to see me. I had never before seen him smile without guile.

"Ella! My dear!"

I didn't care if he was angry. "I ran away from finishing school."

He laughed. "I knew the lass had courage. And are you a lady now or still a clumsy cook's helper?"

"How shall I show you?"

"Curtsy for me."

I swept him my finest.

"Excellent." All his cunning returned. "You are pretty enough. Foolish of me never to have thought of you. Get into the carriage, Eleanor. I trust you will not damage your gown this time."

"Shouldn't we say good-bye to Uaaxee?" I asked, climbing in.

"She won't miss us. She's too heartsore over a gift

from a fairy." He frowned. "They say three were here, and I never saw a hair of them."

The carriage began to move. I didn't care where we were headed.

"You are just in time to put your training to use," Father said.

"Only tell me what I must do."

His eyebrows rose. "This is more transformation than I had hoped for." He was silent for a long while. I began to feel drowsy.

"I am a ruined man."

His voice startled me. "What?"

"I sold an estate that didn't belong to me. The gnomes who bought it have found me out. When we reach Frell, I shall have to repay them, and it will take all I own. I shall have to sell our manor, our furniture, the carriage. And I shall have to sell you, in a manner of speaking. You must marry so that we can be rich again."

So that he could be rich again. "Yes, Father. Gladly. When?" I understood the monstrousness of his plan, but nothing could lessen my joy at the prospect of obeying.

"What did you say?"

"I said, 'Yes, Father. Gladly. When?'"

"You ask when, not to whom? You are so anxious to wed?"

"No, Father. Only to do your bidding."

"What did they do to you at that finishing school? No wonder you ran off."

When we reached our manor, Father stayed outside to speak with the coachman while I hurried inside to find

Mandy. She was scrubbing vegetables, and a parrot perched on her shoulder.

She hugged me so tight, I could barely breathe. "Ella! Ella, my sweet."

The parrot squawked in Gnomic, "!chocH !choe echachoed dh zchoaK !chocH"

I wished she'd never stop squeezing me. I wished I could spend the rest of my life as a child, being slightly crushed by someone who loved me.

Father spoke from the doorway. "I shall be away from home this evening. However, tomorrow we shall entertain. Elvish mushrooms will arrive from the market. They're a delicacy, Mandy. Serve them as a first course for Lady Eleanor and her guest."

"What guest?" Mandy asked after Father left.

"My husband perhaps. I'm so glad, Mandy."

She dropped the pot she'd been washing. It fell into the washtub, but rose back into her hands a moment later. "Your what?"

The parrot squawked again. "!chocH" Mandy had named him Chock, after his favorite word, which was an exclamation in Gnomic meaning "oh," or "oh my," or even "eek!" In this case, I'm sure it meant "eek!"

"My husband. Father has lost all his money. I must marry so he can be rich again."

"This tops all," she stormed. "What is he thinking about, marrying off a chick like you? And why are you glad about it?"

"Not just glad. I'm . . ." I couldn't find the right word. ". . . ecstatic to do it, if it will please them both, my father and my new husband."

Mandy cupped my chin in her hand and examined

my face. "What's happened to you, child?"

"I met Lucinda, and she made me happy to be obedient."

"No, baby. No, honey." Mandy blanched. "She didn't."

"It's much better this way. I don't feel cursed anymore. Don't be sad." I smiled. "See. I'm giving you an order. If you obeyed it, you'd be happy too."

"She turned you from half puppet to all puppet. I'm supposed to be glad about that?"

I didn't answer. While Mandy stood dumbstruck, I looked around the kitchen, greeting every familiar object.

Finally she muttered, "Lucinda's up to new tricks." Then she spoke to me. "I'm starved. Are you ready for dinner, love?"

We supped together in the kitchen, only the two of us and the parrot because Father had dismissed the other servants.

"He must like my cooking too much to get rid of me," Mandy told me over cold chicken wings and warm bread. She spoke no more of my new obedience, but it must have been on her mind, because she changed toward me. She stopped being bossy. I suppose she wouldn't give Lucinda the satisfaction of using my new state. However, Lucinda wouldn't have known, and I was denied the joy of obeying.

The next afternoon we prepared the broth for a fish stew with wild onions—dinner for my guest. I was slicing the onions when a boy brought the mushrooms Father had promised.

Their carton bore the label "torlin kerru." "Kerru"

meant mushrooms, but I didn't know the meaning of "torlin."

Examining the box, Mandy frowned. "Sweet, would you look up that 'torlin' word for me?"

"'Torlin (tor'lin), n., justice; fairness,'" I read in my dictionary. "'Tor'lin ker'ru, justice mushrooms; induce feelings of liking and love in those who eat them; used in elvish courts of law to settle civil disputes.'"

"I'll torlin kerru him!"

"It doesn't matter," I said.

"It matters to me." Mandy yanked on her boots and flung her cloak over her shoulders. "I'll be back soon. Please keep the broth from coming to grief."

I stirred the soup and thought about our dinner guest. I would be glad to marry him, but would I be glad afterward? He might be cruel or dull-witted or mad. Father wouldn't concern himself with my happiness, only with his own.

If he were terrible, Mandy could order me to be contented anyway. Or perhaps I could persuade my husband to issue the command.

Chock landed on my shoulder and pecked lightly at my ear. "!chocH !jdgumkwu azzoogH"

Lovely! An order. I had to kiss him. I turned my head and managed to kiss a wing as he flew to perch on a high shelf.

"!jdgumkwu azzoogH" he squawked again.

I approached the shelf and extended my hand. The bird obligingly hopped on. I brought him close to my face, but before I could touch my lips to a feather, he flew away to the top of a window shutter. I ran for the chair so I could climb up to him, but as soon as I was high enough, he flew off.

When Mandy returned half an hour later, I had a spoon for stirring the broth in one hand and a strainer for catching Chock in the other, and I was breathless from running from one to the other. The curse must have known I was trying to obey, because my complaints hadn't started; I wasn't dizzy or faint or in pain, but I was weeping. Chock wouldn't let me obey and be happy.

"Ella! What's afoot?"

"A-wing! What's a-wing," I corrected, starting to laugh through my tears. "Chock won't let me kiss him."

"Don't kiss the filthy creature," Mandy ordered, releasing me.

"!jdgumkwu azzoogH"

"He did it again," I said.

"Don't kiss him."

",pwoch ech jdgumkwu azzoogH" I told Chock, hoping he'd adopt my addition. I repeated it. ".pwoch ech jdgumkwu azzoogH"

He liked it. ".pwoch ech jdgumkwu azzoogH"

Much better. The new version was "Don't kiss me." I'd be delighted every time he said it.

After we put the kitchen to rights, we began to replace the torlin kerru with innocent mushrooms.

"Maybe I should eat the elvish ones."

"I don't want you hoodwinked even if you don't care."

Father came into the kitchen. "How is our dinner faring?" he asked genially. Then his face darkened. "Why aren't you using my mushrooms, Mandy?"

She dropped a quick curtsy. "I don't know these elvish ones, sir. Maybe they're not fine enough."

I didn't want her to be blamed. "I told her to exchange them when she wasn't sure."

"I sent you to finishing school so you wouldn't be a cook's helper, Ella. Use the elvish mushrooms, Mandy."

CHAPTER NINETEEN

My guest's name was known to me. He was Edmund, Earl of Wolleck, uncle of Hattie's friend Blossom, the uncle whose marriage she feared because it might cause her disinheritance. I suppose I should have been amused, but I was too lost in worry that the uncle would be as unpleasant as the niece.

I waited for him in the study, a half-finished square of embroidery spread across my lap. I had barely seated myself when Father opened the door.

"This is my daughter, Eleanor," he said.

The earl bowed. I stood and curtsied.

He was older than Father, with shoulder-length curled gray hair. His face was as thin as a greyhound's, with a long nose above a drooping mustache. He had a hound's sad eyes too—brown with white showing above the lower lid and bags of skin below.

I sat again and he bent over my handiwork. "Your stitches are neat and so tiny. My mother made the smallest stitches too. You could barely see them."

When he spoke, I saw teeth as small as a baby's, as though he'd never gotten a second set. I could picture the toddler earl, peeking into his mother's lap and flashing those wee pearls at her exquisite embroidery.

When we married, I would try to imagine that he was almost as young as his teeth.

Leaving my side, he turned eagerly to Father.

"You could not hold such a position as I heard you express yesterday, my friend," the earl said. "I hope you will explain yourself more fully."

They were discussing punishments for bandits. The earl thought they should be shown mercy. Father believed they should be treated harshly, put to death even, as an example.

"If a bandit came here and made off with these valuables"—Father waved his hands at the things he was in the process of selling—"I'd be unnatural if I weren't enraged. And unnatural if I didn't act on my rage."

"Perhaps you couldn't help being angry," the earl answered, "but you could certainly stop yourself from repaying one offense with another."

I agreed with the earl and thought of an argument tailor-made for Father. "Suppose the thief didn't steal outright," I said. "Suppose he robbed you through deception. Would that thief deserve the same punishment as a bandit?"

"A different case entirely," Father answered. "If I allowed a rogue to cheat me, I would deserve my fate. The knave would deserve some punishment perhaps, but not a severe one. I would have been a gullible fool and not worthy of my wealth."

The earl nodded at me. "The cases are not so different," he said. "If an armed bandit made off with your possessions, you might be at fault for failing to protect your home. You might then also not be worthy of your wealth. Why should a robber sacrifice his life for your carelessness?"

"Your logic is irrefutable, although its foundation isn't sound." Father smiled. "Two opponents are more than I can defend against. You have much in common with my daughter, Wolleck. You are both soft hearted."

Neatly done, Father. Now the earl and I were a pair.

Dinner was announced. Father led the way to the dining room, leaving the earl to offer me his arm.

The torlin kerru appeared in our first course, as a salad accompanying chilled quail eggs.

"The mushrooms are elf-cultivated," Father said. "Our cook found them in the market and I wanted to serve them to you, although, frankly, I detest fungi. Try them, Ella."

The mushrooms were bland. Their only flavor came from the lemon and sage Mandy had sprinkled on them.

"I'm sorry, Sir Peter," the earl said. "Mushrooms of every variety make me ill. I do enjoy quail eggs, however."

The torlin kerru's effect was rapid. By the time Mandy had whisked away my plate, I was wondering why I had thought the earl resembled a hound when he was really quite handsome. I was liking Father too. By the time we reached the soup course, I was calling the earl "sweet Edmund" in my thoughts and smiling at him after every spoonful. When the fish stew arrived, I suggested to Mandy that she give him an extra ladle.

Father struggled not to laugh.

Even without mushrooms, the earl warmed to me. "Your daughter is charming, Sir Peter," he said during dessert.

"I had no idea she'd grow up so well," he answered. "I must marry her off quickly, or spend all my days looking over her beaux."

Back in the study after dinner, I drew my chair close to the earl. Then I picked up my embroidery and tried to make my stitches so tiny that they *were* invisible.

Edmund and Father were discussing King Jerrold's campaign against the ogres. Father thought the king's knights weren't aggressive enough; the earl believed them to be valiant and praiseworthy.

Although I wanted to pay attention to my sewing, I couldn't. Every time the earl or Father made a point, I nodded my agreement, even though they disagreed.

Then I noticed that the room was chilly and settled back into my seat for warmth.

"Perhaps we should build up the fire, Father. I should hate for our guest to catch cold."

"I've never seen Ella so solicitous," Father said, adding a log to the fire. "She seems enamored of you, Wolleck."

"I am," I murmured.

"What did you say, dear?" Father asked.

Why shouldn't he know how I felt? I wanted him to know. "I am enamored of him, Father," I said clearly, smiling at sweet Edmund. He smiled back.

"This isn't the first time I've sampled Sir Peter's hospitality and his superior table, but you were never here before." He leaned toward me in his chair.

"She was away at finishing school," Father said. "At Madame Edith's establishment in Jenn."

"The time was ill spent," I said, "if it delayed our meeting."

Father blushed.

"My niece, Blossom, is at that school. Were you friends?"

The torlin kerru had no influence over my memory, but I hated to say anything that would cause sweet Edmund pain. "She is several years my senior."

"Blossom is almost eighteen, I think. You can't be very much younger."

"I was fifteen in September."

"You are a child." He drew back in his seat. I couldn't bear it.

"Not such a child," I said. "Mother married when she was sixteen. If I were to die young as she did, I should like first to have lived, and loved."

The earl leaned toward me again. "You have a loving heart. I see that. More woman than child."

Father coughed and offered the earl a brandy. Then he poured a small amount for me.

Edmund touched his glass to mine. "To the eagerness of youth," he said. "May it always get what it longs for."

When he left, he took my hand. "Tonight I came to visit your father. May I return to see you?"

"You cannot come too soon," I said. "Or too often."

When Mandy came to kiss me good night, I told her every word the earl had said after I ate the mushrooms. "Isn't he wonderful?" I asked, wanting her to share my happiness.

"He sounds nice enough," she said grudgingly. "Not like your father, the poisoner."

"But Father is wonderful too," I protested.

"Yes, wonderful!" She slammed the door as she left.

I fell asleep telling myself stories in which I was the heroine and Edmund the hero. But my last conscious idea was an image of Prince Char when he'd caught the bridle of Sir Stephan's horse. His face had been close to mine. Two curls had spilled onto his forehead. A few freckles dusted his nose, and his eyes said he was sorry for me to go.

Mandy woke me when she had finished her work for the night. I was hard to wake. The torlin kerru still had me in their grip.

"I've been pondering. Sweet, think back. Did Lucinda give you a new gift when she made you happy about being obedient?"

"She didn't say." I closed my eyes and pictured our meeting. "She said, 'Obedience is a marvelous gift. . . . Be happy to be blessed with such a lovely quality.' Why?"

"Ah . . . it wasn't a new gift, just an ordinary command. Don't be happy about being obedient, Ella. Be whatever you feel about it."

I was happy to obey. No, I wasn't! The room spun. I began to sob from relief mixed with sadness. I had been a begging puppy and a delighted slave, yet I hadn't felt cursed since I met Lucinda. Now I did again.

After Mandy left me, I fell back to sleep and slept late. When I awoke, my head felt heavy enough to sink through the mattress.

The mushrooms! I bolted up in bed, although my temples throbbed. Every moment of the evening before played in my memory. I pounded the pillow in rage at Father for making such a fool of me.

I found a note on the table next to me.

My dear Eleanor,

You are a charming flirt. Wolleck appeared at dawn to request my permission to declare his intentions to you.

I dropped the letter, afraid to read on. If Father wrote I must marry the earl, I would have to do it. If he came home and told me, I'd have to as well. But before he arrived, I could act. Mandy would tell me the letter's contents without making them an order.

I found her in the henhouse, talking to the chickens.

"Up, Secki."

A hen hopped off its roost, and Mandy collected three eggs.

"Thank you." She went on to the next hen. "Up, Acko. I need only one from you." To me, she said, "Do you fancy an omelette?"

I held the eggs while she read the letter.

"Sounds just like his lordship," she said when she finished. "But it's safe to read."

Father had rejected the earl's suit. Upon close questioning, the earl had confessed that most of his property had recently been consumed by fire. He wasn't rich enough for us.

Poor Blossom. Her inheritance wouldn't be worth much, whether or not the earl married.

Father continued,

I haven't time now to find another suitor. But never fear. I shall secure a rich husband for you yet. For now, however, my own neck will have to go into the noose instead of yours.

There is a lady who will wed me, unless I miss my guess. I have gone to offer her my hand, and to tell her that my heart is already hers. If my suit is successful, I shall send for you so that you may become reacquainted with her.

Reacquainted?

Spare her any tidings of our poverty, although I flatter myself that there is not a shred of greed in Dame Olga's affection for me.

As an accepted suitor or a disappointed lover, I shall see you soon. Until then, and always,

Your father

Dame Olga! Hattie would be my sister!

CHAPTER TWENTY

ame Olga accepted Father's offer. In expressing her satisfaction at gaining a new daughter, she nearly suffocated me.

"My darling, you must call me Mum. Mum Olga sounds so cozy."

The wedding was to be in a week, as soon as arrangements could be made, and as soon as Hattie and Olive returned from finishing school.

"They won't go back after the wedding," Mum Olga said. "They have learned enough. We shall stay here together, and you must all endeavor to lighten my desolation when my husband is away." Her eyes followed Father, who was crossing her parlor to gaze out the window.

"And who will lift my desolation?" he asked, his back to her.

A blush deepened the color in her rouged cheeks. She was besotted with him.

He was all solicitude, all tender attention. She was kittenish, coy, and syrupy. I couldn't be with them for five minutes without wanting to scream.

Fortunately, my presence was required very little. I was rarely invited to Mum Olga's residence, and Father kept her away from our manor, which was day by day being emptied to satisfy his debt.

I cared little about the furniture, except for the fairy rug, which Mandy and I hid one afternoon when Father was with Mum Olga. We also rescued the best of Mother's gowns, because Mandy swore I would shoot up someday soon, and then they would fit me. But we didn't dare touch Mother's jewels. Father would have known if so much as a brass pin had been missing. Anyway, none of them equaled the necklace Hattie had taken from me.

The week was quiet. I spent my days and nights mostly with Mandy. During the day, I helped her cook and clean. At night I read from my fairy book, or we chatted by the kitchen fire.

My only ventures outside were to the royal pastures to see Apple. I had hoped to meet Char there, but the grooms told me he was still chasing ogres.

The first time I visited Apple was the day after I returned to Frell. He stood under a tree, his attention fixed on three brown leaves that clung to a low branch. As I watched, he reared back, lifted his head, and reached for a leaf just beyond his grasp.

In the bunched muscles of his back legs and the straining line from his hips to the tips of his fingers, he was splendid. If Agulen could have seen him, another pottery sculpture would have been born.

I whistled. He whirled and stared at me. I held out a carrot and whistled again, a song about mermaids, Apple's distant cousins. When he saw the treat, he smiled and trotted to me, both hands extended.

Soon, he let me pet his mane and came when I whistled although no food was in sight. It wasn't long before the sight of me inspired as much happiness as a carrot.

I began to confide in him. His wide-eyed attention was an invitation, and his trick of cocking his head to one side while I spoke made me feel that every word was a revelation, although he understood none of it.

"Hattie hates me and makes me do things, never mind why. Olive likes me, which is hardly an advantage. Mum Olga is odious. You and Mandy are the only ones who love me, and you're the only one who will never order me about."

Apple watched my face, his sweet, empty eyes staring into mine, his lips curled into a smile.

The wedding was held in the old castle. Mum Olga wanted it to take place in our manor, but Father said the castle would be more romantic. Against such an argument she had no weapons.

When we arrived, Father went in straightaway to see to details of the ceremony and of the masked ball that would follow. I slipped into the garden to visit the candle trees, which, devoid of their leaves, resembled rows of skeletal arms bent at the elbow.

The day was cold. I passed the candles and marched up and down an avenue of elms, trying not to freeze. I even tied on my mask in a vain attempt to keep my nose warm. No matter how cold I felt, I was going to stay outside until several guests had arrived.

My toes and fingers were numb before I deemed it safe to enter. As soon as I did, Hattie rushed at me, her new false tresses bouncing.

"Ella! I've missed you so!"

She was about to embrace me and, I warrant, whisper a command in my ear.

I stepped away. "If you speak to me at all today, Hattie," I hissed, "I'll snatch off your wig and pass it around to the guests."

"But—"

"Not a word." Taking off my cloak, I walked to the fire and remained there while the buzz of conversation grew behind me.

There was nothing to tempt me to turn. The flames were more interesting than the talk. I wondered what made the air in front of the fire shimmer so.

"Aren't you going to watch the wedding?" Olive knocked my arm. "Can I stay out here with you?"

The hall was silent. I said, "Don't you want to see your mother wed?" I wanted to be there, to see the horrible event.

"I don't care. I'd rather be with you."

"I'm going in."

She followed me, and we slipped into the last row of seats. Father and Mum Olga faced an alcove in which stood High Chancellor Thomas, who had begun to marry them.

His speech sounded familiar, because he'd used almost the same phrases at Mother's funeral. The audience probably could have recited along with him. I heard coughs. A lady ahead of me snored gently, and Olive was soon asleep as well. A man in our row pulled out a knife and cleaned his fingernails.

Only one viewer was rapt, leaning forward in her seat, nodding at each trite sentiment, smiling while dabbing at wet eyes. I smelled lilacs. Lucinda!

She mustn't see me. As the daughter of the groom, I could hardly keep up the pretense that I spoke only

Ayorthaian. She would be livid that I'd fooled her. I put on my mask.

I would leave in the confusion of congratulations when the ceremony ended. I watched her, ready to duck if she turned my way.

As soon as Sir Thomas concluded, Lucinda leaped to her feet. "My friends," she rang out, while advancing on Father and Mum Olga, "never have I been so moved by a ceremony."

Sir Thomas beamed.

"Not because of this man's endless droning . . ."

There were titters.

". . . but because of the love that has united these two, who are no longer in their first youth."

"Madam!" Mum Olga began.

Lucinda didn't hear her. "I am Lucinda, the fairy, and I am going to give you the most wondrous gift."

Mum Olga's voice changed from outrage to delight. "A fairy gift! And everyone here to see! Oh, Sir P., how divine!"

I should have been making my escape, but I stood frozen in place.

Father bowed. "You honor us."

"It's the loveliest gift. No one can say this one is harmful or foolish." She shook her head defiantly. "It's eternal love. As long as you live, you shall love each other."

CHAPTER TWENTY-ONE

Father was open-mouthed in horror.

"It's so romantic, Sir P.," Mum Olga sighed, entwining her arm in his.

His face changed, and he chucked her gently under the chin. "If it pleases you, my dear, my life." He looked wondering. "My love."

Olive climbed over my feet, trumpeting, "A real fairy!" She pushed her way to Lucinda.

Well-wishers crowded around Father and Mum Olga, but few were so foolhardy as Olive. The fairy would soon be free to look about. I fled the room.

It was too cold to hide outdoors. I decided to venture upstairs.

The stair rail was an open spiral, perfect for sliding. I resisted a mad impulse to take a ride—into Lucinda's arms, no doubt. I heard her voice and ran up the stairs.

On the landing I opened a door and stepped into a dark corridor. Closing the door behind me, I sank down and leaned against it with my legs stretched out on marble tiles.

Would Father be happier as a result of the gift? Had Lucinda finally given a present that would benefit its recipients? I tried to imagine their marriage. Would love blind Father to Mum Olga's shortcomings?

There must have been footsteps, but I didn't hear them. The door opened behind me. I tumbled back and found myself staring up at—Char!

"Are you well?" he asked anxiously, kneeling next to me.

I sat up and grabbed his sleeve, scrambling back into the hallway and pulling him with me. I shut the door behind us. "I'm fine."

"Good." He stood up.

I think he was grinning, but he may have been scowling. The corridor was too dim to tell. How would he explain my behavior? Why would he think I was hiding?

"I thought you were still patrolling the border. I didn't notice you at the wedding."

"We returned this morning. I arrived here just in time to watch you dash up the stairs." He paused, perhaps waiting for me to explain. I didn't, and he was too polite to ask.

"My father spent his boyhood here," he went on, "before the new palace was built. He says there's a secret passage somewhere. It's rumored to start in one of the rooms on this story."

"Where does it lead?"

"Supposedly to a tunnel under the moat. Father used to search for it."

"Shall we look?"

"Would you like to?" He sounded eager. "If you don't mind missing the ball."

"I'd love to miss the ball." I opened one of the doors in the corridor.

Light flooded in, and I saw that Char couldn't have

been scowling. He was smiling so happily that he reminded me of Apple.

We were in a bedroom with an empty wardrobe and two large windows. We knocked on the walls, listening for a telltale hollow sound; we felt for hidden seams. We tested the floorboards, guessing at who might have used the passage and for what reasons.

"To warn Frell of danger," Char suggested.

"To escape a mad fairy."

"To flee punishment."

"To leave a boring cotillion."

"That was it," Char agreed.

But whatever the reason for flight, the means remained hidden. We investigated each room less thoroughly than the one before, until our search became a stroll. We moved along the corridor, opening doors and poking our heads in. If any feature seemed promising, we investigated further.

I thought of a silly explanation for my presence upstairs.

"You've guessed why I shut myself up here," I said.

"I have no idea." He opened a door. Nothing worth examining.

"To avoid temptation."

"What temptation?" He grinned, anticipating a joke. He was used to me. I would have to labor to surprise him.

"Can't you guess?"

He shook his head.

"The temptation to slide down the stair rail, of course."

He laughed, surprised after all. "And why were you lying down?"

"I wasn't lying down. I was sitting."

"Pray tell why you were sitting."

"To pretend I was sliding down the stair rail."

He laughed again. "You should have done it. I would have caught you at the bottom."

The strains of an orchestra wafted up to us, a slow allemande.

The corridor we were in ended in a back stair, surrounded by doors that opened on more corridors, all more or less alike.

"If we're not careful, we'll go down this one again," Char said. "They're all the same."

"Hansel and Gretel had pebbles and bread crumbs to show them the way. We have nothing."

"We have more than they did. They were impoverished. There must be something. . . ." He looked down at himself, then tugged at an ivory button on his doublet until it came off in his hand. A bit of striped silk undergarment peeked out. I watched in amazement as he placed the button on the tiles a foot within the hallway we had just left. "That will mark our progress." He chuckled. "I'm destroying my dignity without sliding down anything."

After we investigated six corridors without finding the secret passage, and after all of Char's buttons were gone, we climbed the back staircase. It ended in an outdoor passage to a tower. We rushed across, facing into a bitter wind.

The tower room had once been an indoor garden, with small trees in wooden pots. I perched on a stone bench. It was chilly, but we were out of the wind.

"Do the king's gardeners come here?" I asked. "Are the trees dead?"

"I don't know." Char was staring at the bench. "Stand up."

I obeyed, of course. He pushed at the seat with his foot, and it moved. "This lifts off," he exclaimed.

"Probably only garden tools," I said, while we lifted it together.

I was right, but not entirely. We found a spade, a pail, and a small rake. And cobwebs, and evidence of mice, although how they got in and out I couldn't tell. And a leather apron. And two things more.

Char twitched the apron aside and found gloves and a pair of slippers. The gloves were stained and riddled with holes, but the slippers sparkled as though newly made. Char lifted them out carefully. "I think they're made of glass! Here."

He meant for me to take them both, but I didn't understand. I only reached for one, and the other fell. In the moment before the crash, I mourned the loss of such a beautiful thing.

But there was no crash. The slipper didn't break. I picked it up and tapped on it. The sound was of a fingernail on glass.

"Try them on."

They fit exactly. I held my feet out for Char to see.

"Stand up."

"They'll crack for certain if I do." I could barely stay seated because of the command.

"Perhaps not."

I stood. I took a step. The slippers bent with me. I turned to Char in wonder.

Then I was aware again of the sounds of the orchestra far below. I took a gliding step. I twirled.

He bowed. "The young lady must not dance alone."

I had danced only at school with other pupils or our mistresses for partners.

He put his hand on my waist, and my heart began to pound, a rougher rhythm than the music. I held my skirt. Our free hands met. His felt warm and comforting and unsettling and bewildering—all at once.

Then we were off, Char naming each dance: a gavotte, a slow sarabande, a courante, an allemande.

We danced as long as the orchestra played. Once, between dances, he asked if I wanted to return to the celebration. "Won't they be looking for you?"

"Perhaps." Hattie and Olive would wonder where I was. Father and Mum Olga wouldn't care. But I couldn't go back. Lucinda might still be there. "Do you want to?"

"No. I only came to see you." He added, "To be sure you arrived home safely."

"Quite safely. Sir Stephan guarded me well, and the giants took excellent care of me. Did you catch more ogres?"

"szah, suSS fyng mOOng psySSahbuSS." ("Yes, and they were delicious.")

I laughed. His accent was atrocious.

He shrugged ruefully. "They laughed too and never listened to me. Bertram was the best; they obeyed him half the time."

The music started again, a stately pavane. We could still talk while performing the steps.

"A fairy gave my father and my new mother an unusual gift." I described it. "What do you think of such a present?"

"I shouldn't like to be under a spell to love someone."

Thinking of Father's scheme to marry me off, I said, "Sometimes people are forced into wedlock. If they must marry, perhaps it's better if they must love."

He frowned. "Do you think so? I don't."

I spoke without considering. "It doesn't matter for you. You can marry anyone."

"And you cannot?"

I blushed, furious with myself for almost giving the curse away. "I suppose I can," I muttered. "We're both too young to marry, in any case."

"Are we?" He grinned. "I'm older than you are."

"I am then," I said defiantly. "And the fairy's gift was horrid. I would hate to have to love someone."

"I agree. Love shouldn't be dictated."

"Nothing should be dictated!" An idiotic remark to a future king, but I was thinking of Lucinda.

He answered seriously. "As little as possible."

When the orchestra finished, we sat together on the bench and watched the sky darken slowly.

Sometimes we talked, and sometimes we were silent. He told me more about hunting for ogres. Then he said he was leaving again in two days to spend a year in the court of Ayortha.

"A year!" I knew that the future rulers of Ayortha and Kyrria always spent long periods in each other's courts. The practice had preserved peace for two hundred years. But why now?

He smiled at my dismay. "Father says it's time. I'll write to you. You shall know all my doings. Will you write to me in return?"

"Yes, but I'll have no doings, or few. I shall invent, and you'll have to decide what is real."

The noise of horses and carriage wheels reached us from below, signifying the end of the celebration. I went to a window and looked down. Father and Mum Olga were saying farewell to their guests while Hattie and Olive stood by. Lucinda was at Mum Olga's side.

"The fairy's still here," I said. "Standing at the bride's side."

Char joined me. "Perhaps she means to monitor the effects of her gift."

"Would she? Do you think so?"

"I don't know." He saw my face. "I can tell her to go. She would hardly like a prince for an enemy."

"Don't!" A prince would trouble Lucinda not a whit, and a squirrel prince would trouble her even less. "Let's just watch."

After several more guests departed, Lucinda kissed Father and Mum Olga on the forehead. Then she raised her arms and lifted her head to the twilight sky. For a terrifying moment I thought she saw me. But no, she just smiled her dazzling smile—and vanished.

Char gasped.

I sighed, a long release.

"We'd better go down," I said. "Soon they'll look for me in earnest."

There was just enough light to see by. In a few minutes we stood on the landing above the hall.

"No one is here," Char said. "You need resist temptation no longer."

"Only if you slide too."

"I'll go first so I can catch you at the bottom." He

flew down so incautiously that I suspected him of years of practice in his own castle.

It was my turn. The ride was a dream, longer and steeper than the rail at home. The hall rose to meet me, and Char was there. He caught me and spun me around.

"Again!" he cried.

We raced up. Behind me he said, "Wait till you try the banister at home."

His home! When would I do that?

"Here I go." He was off.

I followed. I was almost to the bottom when the door opened. I sailed into Char's arms observed by the stunned faces of Father and my new family.

Char couldn't see them and twirled me as before, until he got halfway round. Then he set me gently on the floor and bowed at Father and Mum Olga, his buttonless doublet flapping. He was laughing so hard he couldn't speak.

Father grinned. Mum Olga smiled uncertainly. Olive wore her puzzled frown. Hattie glowered.

I used their distraction to conceal the glass slippers in the folds of my skirt.

"Thank you for the honor of your presence," Father said, giving Char time to collect himself.

But not time enough. "You have . . ." Burst of laughter. ". . . my best wishes for your felicity . . ." Laughter. "which is assured. . . ." Peals of laughter. "Forgive me. I'm not laughing . . ." Laughter. ". . . at you. Please understand . . ." He trailed off.

Father chuckled. I laughed helplessly, holding the stair rail for support. I couldn't help it, although I knew Hattie would make me pay.

CHAPTER TWENTY-TWO

After a final awkward bow, Char left us.

"You've made another conquest, Ella," Father said.

"The prince wouldn't—" Hattie began.

I interrupted. "I haven't made any conquests. Your mushrooms made the other one. Besides, soon Ch— the prince leaves to spend a year in Ayortha."

"My darling, must we remain in this drafty hall?" Mum Olga extended her lower lip in an absurd pout.

"Sweetness, you're cold! We'll go at once." Father draped his cloak over Mum Olga's shoulders.

In the coach I was wedged between Hattie and Olive—uncomfortable, but warmed by their bulk. Across from me, Mum Olga turned eagerly to Father.

"Before, it would have been wrong to ask, but now I may, dearest. How rich are we?"

"Why, just as rich as we were before. Silly goose, did you think weddings caused our coffers to grow?" He put his arm around her shoulder.

"No, dear." She pouted again. "I only wanted to know."

"Now you do."

"I may be just a silly goose, but I don't know. I mean, I know how much I have, but I don't know what we have."

Father faced her and put both hands on her shoulders. "My love, you must be brave."

I braced myself.

"I came to you a poor man, with only myself to offer. I hoped it would be enough."

She touched his cheek. "You are just enough for me." Then his words reached her. "Poor? What do you mean poor? Poor is sometimes a figure of speech. Do you mean poor?"

"From my ruin, I salvaged my clothes and Ella's. Little more."

"Mama!" Hattie cried. "I warned you. What will we tell people? I knew Ella—"

She was drowned out by Mum Olga's wails. "Yooou didn't looove meee. Yooou deceeeived meee, myyy looove!"

He drew her against him. She sobbed into his cloak.

"Are we poor?" Olive asked, her voice rising in panic. "Is our money gone? Will we starve?"

"Hush, Olive," Hattie said. "We're not poor. Ella is poor. We must pity her. But—"

She was interrupted. Mum Olga had stopped crying and pushed herself out of Father's arms. She reached across the coach and pawed at me, ripping my reticule from my waist.

"What's in here?" She dumped its contents on her lap. "Coins? Jewels?"

Only a comb and a handkerchief, but she examined the comb. "Silver filigree. I'll keep it." She tossed the purse back at me and then lunged again. The carriage lurched while she clamped onto my bracelet and attempted to pull it off my arm. I tried to push her away, but she held fast.

Father pulled her off me and held her hands in his. "Olga," he said, "we love each other. What else matters? Besides, when I travel again, I'll earn back all I lost and more."

She paid no attention. "I will not have that pauper live like a lady in my house. She can earn her keep."

"Olga, my heart, I expect Ella to be treated with respect," Father said. "She is not to be a servant in her own home. Do you understand, my sweet?"

Mum Olga nodded, but she sent me a look of pure venom.

"Mama, I'd hoped when we were richer we could—"

A footman opened the carriage door. We had arrived at my new home.

My trunk was carried through shadowy hallways to a guest room that was richly furnished but oppressively dark. The chambermaid lit three lamps, which illuminated but did not lighten the effect. She turned down the bedclothes and left me.

I wished Mandy could come in to say good night, but she wouldn't arrive from our old home until the next day. I was alone with my fears. What would happen to me here? How would Mum Olga punish me for Father's deception? And how soon would Hattie resume her tyranny over me?

I didn't have long to wait for Hattie. She issued her first order the next day. She gave it when one of the menservants announced that Char had come calling. He'd come to see me, but she told me to keep to my room while she entertained him.

"You'll only be in my way, dear."

"He wants me. You'd be in my way."

"Go to your room, Ella." She patted Mother's necklace. "The prince belongs to me too."

In my room, I banged on the floor, hoping Char would come to investigate the noise. But the walls and floors were too thick for him to hear me.

Afterward she said, "At first he may have wanted to see you, but I won him over. When he bid me goodbye, he said our conversation would stay in his memory forever."

He came the next day too, and I was again confined to my room.

I passed half the time of his visit standing at my door, trying to force myself to emerge from the room and from the curse. The other half I spent at the window, watching for him. When he left, he glanced back for a final view of our manor. I started to wave, but he turned away.

An entry from his journal appeared in my magic book the night he left for Ayortha. He had seen me.

Ella is avoiding me. Twice I visited her house, only to be told she was out calling. On both days her stepsister Hattie said Ella would return shortly, so I waited for hours, but she never came.

When I gave up yesterday, I looked back for a last glimpse of her manor, since I couldn't have a last glimpse of her. But there she was, standing at an upstairs window.

I should have returned immediately and insisted on seeing her, but I was too confused. Why was she there? Was she hiding from me? Was she angry? If she was, she should have come into the drawing room and told me. I thought her forthright enough to do so.

I resolved to visit again in the evening and demand to see her. But when I got home, Mother had a surprise family party waiting to bid me farewell and I couldn't leave. This morning I would have gone too, but Father was impatient to be off, and there was no delaying him.

Perhaps she's embarrassed about sliding down the stair rail and blames me for encouraging her. Perhaps her father and his new wife were displeased.

I had wanted to tell her about the afternoon I spent flying down the stair rails at home, never noticing the gradual shredding of my breeches.

That would have made her laugh. She makes me laugh so easily, I always wish to return the favor.

Instead, I had to listen while Hattie chattered endlessly. I don't know how she managed to pour the words out while smiling so hard, revealing the largest teeth I've ever seen. She must be excellent at cracking nuts. This is unkind of me. Her teeth are on the large side, nothing exceptional.

The younger stepsister, Olive, said little, but the little was astonishing. She wanted to know whether people had to give me their wealth if I told them to. When I asked her why I'd want to take my subjects' money, she was surprised. "To become richer," she said as though stating the obvious.

All this I endured while Ella hid. And now I won't see her again for a year.

I had to write to him. If he thought I was angry, he might never write to me. But how could I explain my behavior?

The guest room I occupied was supplied with writing

paper, ink, and a pen. I trimmed the pen, then found I didn't know how to begin. I could call him "Char" quite easily, but writing it was another matter. "Dear Char" looked disrespectful on the page. "Dear Prince Charmont" or "Dear Highness" seemed too formal. And how would I conclude? "Yours truly" and "Sincerely" seemed stiff, while "Your friend" seemed childish.

Omitting the salutation, I began. It would be addressed to him, so there should be no mistake.

I have been confined to my room. I saw you come to visit and saw you leave. I waved, but you must not have seen. Father is vexed with me. It has nothing to do with you. He was insulted that I left the wedding early.

Two more days remain to my sentence. Now that you are gone and I can no longer hope to tell you good-bye, it is not so terrible. I hope you will still write to me, and not only about Ayortha. I have many questions, most of them impertinent. When you were a boy, did you study with other children, or did you have tutors all to yourself? I suppose you were equally wonderful at all your subjects—but were you? Who took care of you when you were small? When did you discover you were a prince and would someday be king? What did the knowledge mean to you?

If my questions offend, please do not answer any of them.

I went on to tell him about my years before Mother died, games with Mother and Mandy, the taste of Tonic, listening to fairy stories. I omitted only the most important facts: Lucinda's gift and that Mandy was a fairy.

Then I promised,

In my next letter, I shall tell more about finishing school and the elves and Areida, my Ayorthaian friend. If you write quickly, I shall also send Mandy's and my recipe for roly-poly pudding. (Cooking is another of my accomplishments, although not taught at finishing school.) You may try the recipe and astound your hosts.

If you do write, pray do not address the letters to me or mark them to show that you are the correspondent. Direct your letters to Mandy. She'll see that I get them.

You are shocked that I have proposed a subterfuge. My only hope is that one who flies down a stair rail as beautifully as you do can overcome his scruples in this matter.

As my Ayorthaian friend would say, "Adumma ubensu enusse onsordo!" Or, please write soon.

I closed with, "Your impatient friend, Ella." Somehow, the adjective made the rest less childish. I went back to the beginning and added "Dear Char" as the salutation.

But how was I to address the letter? I had no idea where he was staying.

In the end, I directed it to the royal family in Ayortha and prayed it fell into helpful hands.

Now, I could only wait for a reply. In the meanwhile, what would I have to endure from my stepfamily?

CHAPTER TWENTY-THREE

Three days after Char left, Father went too, off to be a merchant again. Before leaving, he spoke to me privately in the small parlor he had converted into his study.

"I leave at noon," he said. "Thank heaven the fairy left me my will and my reason so that I can leave, although I shall long for my Olga every moment I'm gone. What a gift! If I could take this knife"—he touched the scabbard at his waist—"and carve out the part of my heart that belongs to my wife, I should do it."

He would never hurt himself. "Why must I stay with them?" I asked.

"Where else can you go? You fled finishing school, and you'll be in better society here than you would find with me. Including me. Don't run off again."

"You are better society than they are," I said. It was true: There was a little honesty in Father but none at all in Hattie or Mum Olga.

"This is praise indeed. Come, tell your father good-bye."

"Farewell."

"I shall miss you, child." He kissed my forehead. "I prefer to love my wife from afar. I shall not soon return."

"I don't care."

But I found that I did.

As soon as Father's carriage disappeared from view, Mum Olga swallowed her tears and directed a manservant to transfer my belongings to a room in the servants' wing.

With a tiny window and no fireplace, it was more cell than room, just large enough for a pallet on the floor and a small wardrobe. It was cold now in late November. In winter it would be a chamber of ice.

After my things were moved, Mum Olga sent for me. Hattie and Olive were with her in the rear parlor that faced the garden. I took a seat near the door.

"You are not to sit in the presence of your betters, Ella."

I didn't move.

Mum Olga sputtered. "Did you . . ."

"Stand, Ella," Hattie commanded.

I fought for a moment, then rose.

Hattie put her arm around my shoulders. "Ella will be obedient, Mama. Tell Mama how obedient you'll be."

"Very obedient," I mumbled while grinding my heel into her toe.

She yelped in pain.

"What is the meaning of this?" Mum Olga asked.

"The meaning, Mama, is that Ella does whatever she is told. I don't know why, but she does."

"Really?"

Hattie nodded.

"You mean she would have listened to me too?" Olive said.

"Clap your hands three times, Ella," Mum Olga commanded.

I clutched my skirts and stiffened my hands at my sides.

"It will take a moment," Hattie said. "She tries not to. See how red her face is."

I clapped.

"What a clever daughter I have." Mum Olga beamed at Hattie.

"As clever as she is beautiful," I said.

They both began to answer me and stopped, confused.

"Hattie isn't pretty," Olive said.

Mum Olga rang her bell. In a few minutes, two housemaids entered the room, followed by Mandy and the rest of the servants.

"From now on, Ella will be one of you," Mum Olga said. "Teach her to be a good servant."

"I'll take her for my helper," the laundress said.

I stifled a cry. On my first day in Mum Olga's manor, I'd seen the laundress blacken the eye of a housemaid.

Mandy spoke up. "I need a scullery maid. I know the lass. She's stubborn, but trainable. May I have her, your ladyship?"

Since the wedding, Mum Olga had been eating Mandy's cooking, in ever-increasing helpings. By now, she would probably have given Mandy fifty scullery maids to keep her happy.

"Are you certain you want her, if she's so obstinate?"

"I'll take her," Mandy answered. "The chit means nothing to me, but I loved her mother. I'll teach her to cook, and your ladyship can train her for other service, but I'll allow no harm to come to her, if your ladyship takes my meaning."

Mum Olga puffed up to her full height and girth. "Are you threatening me, Mandy?"

"No, mistress. Bless me, no. I want to keep my situation. But all the fine cooks in Kyrria are my friends, and if anything happened to the wench, I don't know who would cook for you."

"I won't have her spoiled."

"Spoiled! I'll work her harder than she ever worked in her life, and give you a fine cook into the bargain."

The bargain was irresistible.

Midmorning of my second day of servitude, Olive joined us in the kitchen.

"I'm hungry," she said, although breakfast had been only an hour earlier. "Make me a white cake."

Mandy began to assemble the ingredients.

"No, I want Ella to do it." She stood at my side while I measured and mixed. "Talk to me."

"What should I say?"

"I don't know. Anything."

I told her a fairy tale about a prince with a long nose who loved a princess with a short nose. The tale had humor and grief, and I enjoyed telling it. Over her cooking, Mandy chuckled and sighed at the proper moments. But Olive only listened silently, her eyes riveted on my face.

"Tell me another," she said when I announced the end, suspecting she wouldn't recognize it otherwise.

I recited "Beauty and the Beast." My mouth was getting dry. I pumped water into a cup.

"Give me some too," she demanded.

I refilled the cup. Was I going to pass the rest of my life catering to this . . . this . . . this *appetite*?

"Another story," she said when she finished drinking. She said the same after "Rapunzel" and "Hansel and Gretel." Before she could order one more after the tale of King Midas, I asked her hoarsely if she'd liked the story.

She nodded, and I persuaded her to tell it back to me. "A king turns everything into gold and lives happily ever after. I want more."

Not a command. "I've told every story I know."

"I want money." Perhaps she was thinking about Midas. "Give me your money."

I had gotten only a few KJs from Father before he went away, which I hoped to keep in case of need.

"Don't you want Ella to finish making your cake?" Mandy asked. "I thought you were hungry."

"No! I want her money." Olive's voice rose.

Mandy tried again. "What does a rich young lady such as yourself want with the wee savings of a scullery maid?"

"To make me richer. Mother and Hattie have much more than I do." She started to wail. "It's not fair."

My head hurt from not obeying, as well as from Olive's noise. I pushed the mixing bowl away. "Come with me."

My money was in my room, at the bottom of my carpetbag. I hunted through it without letting Olive see my Agulen wolf or my glass slippers. She probably wouldn't have recognized their value, but she might have talked about them to her mother or to Hattie.

I had only three silver KJs, enough to buy a few meals or a night at an inn. Olive counted them twice.

"I have to put them away." She closed her fists over them and marched off.

I was penniless, stripped of the power that even a few coins bestow.

For a quarter hour I sat on my bed, enjoying the quiet and trying fruitlessly to think of new ways to break the curse. Then I returned to the kitchen to help Mandy with lunch. When I entered, Olive was there.

"Talk to me," she said.

In the evening, there was to be a formal dinner to console Mum Olga for Father's departure. I had to wash the floor in the hall in preparation while Mum Olga came by frequently to supervise.

"You must scrub on your knees, and add lye to the water. It scours best."

As soon as I submerged my hands, they smarted and burned. I drew them out of the bucket.

"Don't stop before you've started. The dinner is tonight, not next week."

The task took three hours, but my knuckles were bleeding in a quarter of the time. Occasionally other servants passed by. Some gawked, some seemed sympathetic. Nancy, the serving maid, came during one of Mum Olga's inspections. She crept behind Mum Olga and pantomimed dumping a pail of water over her head.

"Something amuses you?" Mum Olga asked.

I shook my head and stopped smiling.

At last I finished. In addition to bloody hands, my knees were bruised, and my arms ached. I wished I were a real servant, the sort who could quit one situation and seek another.

I returned to help Mandy in the kitchen. Fortunately, she was alone. As soon as she saw me, she rushed to her store of herbs and unguents and to the jug of Tonic.

"Sit down, sweet. I'll have you good as new in a minute."

Her remedies worked miracles, but better yet, during dinner I had revenge. Mandy had just sprinkled parsley over thirty servings of trout, and Nancy was ready to convey them to the guests.

"Wait!" I dashed to the herb cabinet. "Here." I scattered ground passiflora over one of the plates. "Give this one to my stepmother."

"What . . ." Nancy looked startled.

"Don't do it," Mandy said. "I won't have her ladyship blaming me when she starts snoring in front of her guests."

"Oh, is that all? Serve her right." Nancy took the plate and was off.

"A good lass, Nancy," Mandy said, grinning at me when she had gone.

Two servants had to carry Mum Olga to bed before the meal ended. But the festivities continued, culminating in dancing. I witnessed the dance because Hattie called me to tend the fire, and everyone saw me in my greasy, sooty state.

Afterward, while I undressed in my room, I thought about escape. Mandy would only use small magic, which was smaller help than I needed. And Char was hundreds of miles away and mustn't know of my troubles anyway.

Father. I hated to ask him for anything, but he was the only one who could help. I would write to him.

CHAPTER TWENTY-FOUR

In my letter I played on Father's pride and described the part of my servitude that would most enrage him: tending the fire in front of the courtiers.

How dare they treat me so. And against your express wishes too! They order me about, and the more menial the task, the better.

I beg you to come home. Many merchants trade right here in Frell; why can't you join their number? Please come. My need is great. You know I would not ask otherwise. Come quickly. I am counting the days.

Your daughter,
Ella

I gave the letter to Mandy to post. Perhaps it would overtake Father on the road. The mail coach driver knew him. It might reach him before my earlier letter got to Char. Father could even be back in a few days.

Until I saw him or heard from him, I would endure. I stayed out of my stepfamily's way as much as possible, and the longer I worked as a scullery maid, and the filthier I got, the less Hattie and Mum Olga tormented me. I think they gloried in my squalor as proof of my baseness.

From Olive, though, there was no respite, and to escape from her, I hid. My most secure hideaway was the library. Although I never dared stay long, I was able to steal half hours reading Mum Olga's dusty tomes. No one ever thought to look for me there, or to visit for pleasure.

I don't know whether I was more anxious to hear from Father or from Char. I kept thinking about Char and wishing to talk to him. If I thought of a joke, I wanted to try it on him. If I had a serious idea, I wanted his opinion.

Although weeks passed without an answer from Father, my first letter from Char arrived only ten days after I'd sent mine to him. Then letter followed letter for the first six months of his absence, while I heard nothing from Father, and saw nothing of him either.

As I had directed, Char sent his letters to Mandy, who pretended to have an admirer. Hattie and Mum Olga were vastly amused at Mandy's romance, but I failed to see why it was any more absurd than Mum Olga and Father.

Char's hand was large and round, the letters evenly spaced, each fully formed—completely unlike my crabbed, spiky writing. His showed a balanced, honest nature, while Areida used to say mine proved me imaginative, impulsive, and always in a hurry.

Dear Ella,

My name has been changed. Here they call me Echarmonte, which sounds more like a sneeze than a name. They can't pronounce Char, and I can't persuade them to call me Echare. They are so formal. They say "by your leave" more often than they say anything else.

The Ayorthaians think before they speak, and often conclude, after lengthy meditation, that nothing need be said. The loudest beings in an Ayorthaian council are the flies. The occasional bee that finds its way in is deafening.

I long for conversation. The ordinary Ayorthaians are talkative, but the nobles are not. They are kind. They smile easily. But speech for them is a single word, occasionally a phrase. Once a week they utter a complete sentence. On their birthdays they grant the world an entire paragraph.

At first I chattered to fill the silence. In response, I received smiles, bows, thoughtful expressions, shrugs, and an occasional "Perhaps, by your leave." So now I keep my speeches to myself.

In the garden this morning I overtook the duke of Andona. I touched his shoulder in greeting. He nodded companionably. In my mind I said, "The flowers are marvelous. That one grows in Kyrria, but that other I've never seen before. What do you call it?"

In my imagination he answered me, naming the flower, saying it was the queen's favorite and that he'd be happy to give me seeds.

But if I had really asked about a flower, he'd probably have continued strolling. He'd have thought, "Why does this prince clutter up a lovely day with talk? If I don't answer him, he may breathe in the sweet air, feel the gentle sun, hear the rustling leaves. Perhaps by now he regrets his question. But perhaps he thinks me rude for not answering him. However, if I speak now, I may startle him. Which would be worse? It would be worse to have *him think me rude. I must speak." But, exhausted by his cogitation, he'd have energy left for only one word, the name of the flower.*

I'm writing nonsense. In my first letter I had hoped to impress you with my brilliant prose, but that will have to wait for my second.

Not many of my imagined conversations are with the duke. Most of them are with you.

I know what I would say if I were in Frell. I'd tell you at least three times how glad I was to see you. I'd speak more about Ayortha (and with fewer complaints), and I'd describe my trip here, especially our adventure when one of the packhorses shied at a rabbit and tore off. But then I might turn Ayorthaian and trail off into silence, lost in smiling at you.

The trouble is, I can't guess at your response. You surprise me so often. I like to be surprised, but if I could supply your answers with confidence, I might miss you less. The remedy is obvious. You must write to me again and quickly. And again, and more quickly.

Your very good friend,
Char

In my reply, I gave him conversation.

Greetings. How do you fare today? Lovely weather we've been having. The farmers predict rain, however. They say the crows are chattering. Ah well, wet weather will do us good, I daresay. We can't have sunny days always. Life isn't like that, is it? Wish it were. Wouldn't that be fine? Never a disappointment, never a harsh word.

Don't you agree, sir? A fine fellow such as yourself, you have sense enough to see it's never that way.

In one dose, I hope I have cured you of your desire for conversation.

My pen stopped. What could I tell him? I couldn't explain my servitude without telling about the curse. Then I recollected that Mum Olga had recently held a cotillion. I described it, omitting the detail that my participation had been limited to removing the dirty plates from the refreshments table.

Char's reply was that the Ayorthaians didn't have balls.

They have "sings," which are held monthly. Three or four Ayorthaians at a time occupy the stage in turn and sing long, sad ballads or happy tunes or funny ones, joined by the whole throng in the choruses. The entire populace knows thousands of songs, and there is hardly a mediocre voice among them.

Sound gushes forth from somewhere deep, their toes or their souls. For the last song, a paean to the rising sun (because they have performed through the night), they gather their families about them. Husbands and wives and children clasp hands, tilt their heads heavenward, and release their music.

And I, seated with the few other visitors, add my weak voice to theirs, humming when I can't guess the words and wishing my hands were held too.

Perhaps we can come here together someday.

By the way, you are a month older than the last time I saw you. Are you still too young to marry?

I chuckled at the joke. Then I thought of the bride I'd make, in a threadbare, sooty gown that stank of cooking fat and yesterday's dinner.

Char repeated the query in every letter, probably because my answers were so silly that they pleased him. If not too young, I was too tired to marry or too wet or too cross or too hungry. Once I wrote, "If my years are measured by inches, then I am certainly too young. The eleven-year-old daughter of an acquaintance dwarfs me."

The acquaintance was Nancy, the serving maid.

Another time I wrote, "Today I am too old to marry, a hundred at least. I have spent the last eighty years and more listening to a lady detail the pedigree of every dinner guest tonight."

The lady had been Hattie, and I had not attended the meal.

I continued in a more serious vein. "I have not found anyone in my stepfamily's circle in whom I can confide. And there are few subjects about which my stepsisters and I share an opinion. It is great good luck that I have a pen and paper and a friend."

Char's answer: "My tongue may wither from disuse here, but at least I shan't lose words entirely while I still can write to you."

Sometimes I wondered what would happen if I told Char that I was just the right age to marry. With each of his letters I fell more in love with him. But I couldn't tell him. If I said I was old enough to marry and his question had only been the continuation of a good joke, he would be horribly embarrassed and our easy friendship would be ruined. He might stop writing, which I couldn't endure. If he wasn't jesting, it was for him to say so. Until then or never, I treasured our correspondence.

In his next letter he wrote,

I don't know when I learned I would be king. It seems I've always known it. But two stories are told, and I've heard them so often they seem to be memories. One has me as hero; the other is not so flattering.

A lute was given to me when I was six and my sister, Cecilia, was four. She coveted it and plucked at it whenever she could. Finally, I presented it to her, an act that signified to the servants that I would be a generous king. They never considered how indifferent a musician I was. My protestations that it was a small sacrifice to part with something I had little use for were taken as modesty, another fine kingly quality.

However, I'm not sure how modesty figures in my retelling the tale to you. I do so because I want you to know I have qualities that others admire. What you will conclude from the next anecdote I cannot guess.

I was in the streets of Frell with my father when a man pelted him with an overripe tomato. While wiping at his clothes, my father spoke kindly to the man and ended by resolving his grievance. Afterward, I asked why the man hadn't been punished. When Father told me I'd understand by the time I became king, I said I didn't want to be king if people threw tomatoes at me. I said it seemed a thankless task.

Father roars with laughter when he tells this tale. Now I know why: It is a thankless task, but tomatoes are the least of it.

The conclusion I drew from this story was that Char wasn't above laughing at himself. Of course, he wasn't perfect. Eager to share his knowledge on any subject, he neglected to ascertain the interest of his listener or, in my case, reader. He wrote more about Ayortha than I ever wished to know: how the guilds were structured; the number of gallons of milk produced in a year by one Ayorthaian cow; the construction of their manors. And yet more.

This was a minor flaw. He confessed a more serious one.

You are almost my sole confidant in this. The other is my horse, to whom I tell everything—because he can't condemn or offer advice. I write it to you because you must know all. I trust you to find the good in me, but the bad I must be sure you don't overlook.

I am slow to anger, but also slow to forgive. For example, my languages tutor had a way of making me feel a fool. I endured his abuse but learned less than I might have if he'd been encouraging. Cecilia, who inherited his instruction after me, received the same treatment. The first time I found her crying, I warned him. The second time, I dismissed him. Father trusted my judgment enough to let my action stand.

I went further. Boy as I was, I took measures to ensure the tutor would teach no more. But although my victory was complete and the man was ruined, and six years have passed, the thought of him still infuriates me. I am angry now as I write these words.

You may excuse me on the grounds of being a kind

brother, which I hope I am. But I wonder at my rage. And I wonder too if my action against the tutor was at bottom a case of refusing (in another form) to let someone throw a tomato at me or my family.

In reply I wrote,

Mandy says there are two sorts of people in the world: those who blame everyone else and those who blame only themselves. I place myself in a third category: among those who know where blame really lies. You stand condemned. Your crime: too much zeal in the protection of those you love. A fault and a virtue. Heinous!

Although you've revealed your shortcomings to me, I feel compelled to no such frankness. You must discover my faults for yourself. And, although you've said it goes against the grain, you must find a way to forgive them.

I remember the date of Char's next letter: Thursday, May 24. He'd been gone half a year. Although the letter arrived in the morning, I was unable to read it all day. At dawn I had to scrub the flagstones in our courtyard for Mum Olga. Then Olive ordered me to count her coins in their thousands—repeatedly, because she kept thinking I had made a mistake. In the evening Hattie had me help her prepare for a ball, including plucking out the hairs that grew in profusion above her upper lip.

By the time Hattie departed, I was too late to help Mandy clean the kitchen. The rest of the night was mine to use as I liked.

In my room I opened my little window and let the cool air wash over me. Then I lit the bit of candle

Mandy had smuggled to me, placing it carefully out of the breeze. I sat on my cot and opened my letter.

Dear Ella,

Impatience is not usually my weakness. But your letters torment me. They make me long to saddle my horse and ride to Frell, where I would make you explain yourself.

They are playful, interesting, thoughtful, and (occasionally) serious. I'm overjoyed to receive them, yet they bring misery. You say little of your daily life; I have no idea how you occupy yourself. I don't mind; I enjoy guessing at the mystery. But what I really long to know you do not tell either: what you feel, although I've given you hints by the score of my regard.

You like me. You wouldn't waste time or paper on a being you didn't like. But I think I've loved you since we met at your mother's funeral. I want to be with you forever and beyond, but you write that you are too young to marry or too old or too short or too hungry—until I crumple your letters up in despair, only to smooth them out again for a twelfth reading, hunting for hidden meanings.

Father asks frequently in his letters whether I fancy any Ayorthaian young lady or any in our acquaintance at home. I say no. I suppose I'm confessing another fault: pride. I don't want him to know that I love if my affections are not returned.

You would charm him, and Mother too. They would be yours completely. As I am.

What a beautiful bride you'll be, whomever you marry at whatever age. And what a queen if I am the man! Who has your grace? Your expression? Your voice? I could extol your virtues endlessly, but I want you to finish reading and answer me quickly.

Today I cannot write of Ayortha or my doings or anything. I can only post this and wait.

Love (it is such relief to pen the word!), love, love—

Char

CHAPTER TWENTY-FIVE

I gaped at the page. Read it again. And gaped again. In my daze, I noticed that my sooty thumb had left marks on the letter.

He loved me. He'd loved me as long as he'd known me!

I hadn't loved him as long, perhaps, but now I loved him equally well, or better. I loved his laugh, his handwriting, his steady gaze, his honorableness, his freckles, his appreciation of my jokes, his hands, his determination that I should know the worst of him. And, most of all, shameful though it might be, I loved his love for me.

Placing my candle carefully, I danced and whirled around my room.

I could marry Char and live with my love.

I could leave Mum Olga and her spawn.

No one would give me orders.

This was an unexpected solution to my trouble. Lucinda would have hated for me to evade my obedience by rising above it. And even Mandy would be surprised by this method of ending the curse.

I extracted paper from the hiding place at the bottom of my wardrobe. My love shouldn't have an extra moment of impatience.

However, my stub of a candle flickered out as soon as I wrote, "Dearest Char, darling Char, beloved Char."

I ordered my mind to wake me the instant there was light enough to write by. Then I fell asleep composing my letter.

In the middle of the night, I awoke, my happiness draining away. I wouldn't escape the curse by marrying Char. I would be more cursed than ever. And he would be cursed too.

Suppose my obedience were discovered . . . My step-family knew and would take advantage to improve their rank and fortune. But that would be the least of it—an enemy of Kyrria could put the curse to more awful use. In unscrupulous hands I would be a powerful tool. I could be made to reveal state secrets. I could even be forced to kill Char!

And I had no doubt my secret would be discovered. In court there would be eyes and ears that would be alive to such signs. I'd never manage to fool them all.

What could I do? Mother had ordered me not to tell anyone about the curse, but Mandy could countermand the order so I'd be able to tell Char. Then he could take precautions.

I'd tell him. I'd wake Mandy now. I sat up in bed, happy again. And sank back.

What precautions could Char take? He could prevent anyone from speaking to me or writing to me. He could shut me away. That might do, but he would have to bring me my meals, the flax to spin my clothes, the wood for my fire. It would be a burden similar to one of Lucinda's wedding gifts. And what would Kyrria think of a hermit queen? And how would I feel, locked away like Rapunzel in her tower? Moreover, even the best precautions might fail.

I could ask him to give up being crown prince in favor of his sister. If he were never to be king, he might not be a target. But how could I ask such a thing? How could he accept? And would the danger simply move to his sister?

We could keep the marriage a secret. That was absurd. The secret would get out.

I cast about for other ideas, but none came. Cursed, I couldn't marry him. But if I ever managed to break the curse, in a month or in twenty years, I would find him and win him over again if he was still free. No matter what I had to do, no matter how long it took. But now my only choice was to convince him to give me up.

When I finally thought what to say and began to write, I ruined three sheets of paper by crying on them and a fourth because I forgot to misspell words.

My dear Prince Charmont,

Your latest corespondence with my stepsister was recieved by my mother, Dame Olga, and myself. Ella and the cook, Mandy, were not here to except it.

Ella is absent because she has eloped, taking our cook with her. She left a note which I have enclosed for your perusal.

You have been much decieved in her. It was her custom to read your letters aloud to us and crow over them, thinking it a feather in her cap to be writing to royalty, such as yourself.

For a while, she had ambitions to be queen, but she dispared of it and took another offer. She would go into one of her dreadful rages if she knew the contents of your letter. I do not think she liked living on our generosity, and longed to be able to lord it over us with greater splendor than we could hope for, although we fancy that our stile is very fine.

Your letter arrived four days after her departure. I know because Demby had a ball that night, and Ella was greatly missed. Her beaux turned to me for consolation, and I gave them the same advice I have for you: Think no more of the minks, because she has already forgotten you.

I am sorry to dismay you, but I hope you will be consoled by the fond wishes of this admirer.

Your angel of comfort,
Hattie

I tore a sheet of paper in half for the enclosure, written in my own hand.

These are the first words I ever penned as a married lady. You know him, but I shall not write his name, only that he is very old and very rich and lives far from Frell. And he is fool enough to make me his bride. Someday, and the day may not be long in coming, I shall be sole mistress of a vast estate. I shall not write again, but look for me. When my husband dies, I shall visit Frell. Should you spy a carriage that surpasses all others, peer inside. You will find me within, smiling at my jewels and laughing at the world—

Ella

Char's anger at his tutor would be nothing compared with this. He would hate me until the end of the world.

ঙ

In the morning, Mandy dispatched the correspondence, thinking it an ordinary letter. I didn't tell her about Char's proposal for fear she would think I should accept him. Although I knew I was right, I doubted I could withstand any argument.

As soon as she left to post the letter, I collapsed in front of the fireplace, sobbing. When she returned in half an hour, I was still in tears.

She gathered me in her arms. "What's the trouble, sweet?"

For a few minutes I continued to cry too hard to speak. When I was able to control myself, I told her. "Did I do right?" I asked at the end.

"Come with me, Lady." She grabbed my hand and half dragged me to her room, passing several servants in the hall. Once there, she closed the door and turned to me. "Lady, you did right. Now I'm going to do right, something I should have done long ago. Get behind the curtains, love."

I hesitated, pushing back the urge to obey. "Why?"

"I'm going to settle scores of scores with Lucinda. I want you to see me do it, but I don't want her to see you."

I hid.

"Lucinda! I need you."

The scent of lilacs filled the room. I stifled a gasp. I could see Lucinda's outline through the rough weave of the draperies.

"I never thought the day would come when the kitchen fairy would call me. I'm delighted. How can I help you, dear?"

"Don't 'dear' me." Mandy sighed. "But you're right. I need your help."

"And I love to help."

Safely hidden, I grimaced at her.

"I've been gathering my courage to ask you ever since the fairy ball."

"One has only to ask."

Mandy sounded regretful. "At the ball I got into an argument with Kirby."

"You shouldn't have. I never argue."

"But I do. It was about you. Kirby said we should suggest you try being a squirrel and try being obedient. If you gave it a fair trial—three months as a squirrel, three as an obedient human—you'd find out that your gifts aren't so wondrous after all."

"I don't have to try out my gifts to know they're magnificent."

"That's what I said you'd say. There, I can tell Kirby I won the argument. I said you'd be too afraid you were wrong to put it to the test."

Lucinda vanished. She must have been too angry at Mandy to continue the discussion. But then Mandy laughed. "Don't forget to be obedient, little one. Here's a nice walnut. I'm sending you to a comfortable park." She paused. "You can come out, Lady."

"Did she really turn herself into a squirrel?" I emerged cautiously.

"She did." Mandy was still laughing.

"Do you think she'll learn?"

"If she doesn't, she's even more of a blockhead than I think."

"What if an animal eats her?"

"If that happened, I'd fear for the animal." She chuckled. "What a stomachache it would have."

"If she learns her lesson, will she undo all her gifts?"

"I don't know. I just had to stop her mischief. You may yet break the curse yourself."

"But if she discovers how wrong she was, she'll want to lift the spell."

"Maybe. But it would be more big magic." Mandy drew me into a hug. "Oh, love, I know what that spell does to you."

I pushed out of her arms. "You don't know! And how can you warn against big magic when you just summoned Lucinda?"

"Nothing one fairy does to another is big magic, Lady."

"Stop calling me 'Lady.' You used to call Mother that."

"Now you're a lady too. If you'd put yourself first and married the prince, someone would have come along to harm him and Kyrria, sure as cabbages. You're a heroine, sweet."

"I'd rather be his wife." The tears welled up again, and I threw myself across Mandy's bed.

She sat next to me, stroking my back and murmuring. "Oh, sweet, my Lady. Perhaps it will come right." She shifted her weight. Something crackled, and she exclaimed, "What's this? Oh, I forgot! When I posted your letter, there was one for you." She pulled a letter out of her apron pocket.

I flew up.

"It's not in the prince's hand, love."

It was from Father, saying he wouldn't come home.

My servitude pained him, but not enough to return him to the arms of his odious, though beloved, wife. He wrote, "When I find a husband for you who is rich enough to satisfy me, you will be released from my Olga. Until then, I urge you to be, as always, my stalwart daughter."

I fell back on the bed, laughing wildly. Father would make my letter to Char come true. He would marry me off to an ancient man who would soon die and leave me enormously wealthy. The irony! I couldn't catch my breath. Tears ran down my face, and I didn't know whether I was laughing or crying.

Mandy held me until I quieted. While she rocked me, I thought that Lucinda still might save me. Mandy might be wrong. Once Lucinda knew how it was to be obedient, she wouldn't be able to leave me cursed. She'd have to help me.

A week later I saw in my magic book that Char had received my message. I opened to an illustration in which he was burning my letters. I was glad to see his image, no matter what the image was doing.

After I gazed awhile and ran my fingers over his shape, I turned the page and found an entry in his journal.

I've lost nothing. She never was what I thought her, so I've lost nothing. I'm only fortunate, and Kyrria is blessed, that she eloped before my letter reached her.

When I received the message from her sister, I thought it had to be a ploy to make me hate Ella, and I resolved not to be taken in. For a while I considered leaving Ayortha to discover the truth. Gradually, however, I realized the truth was in my hands.

The sister could have no reason to lie to me. If Ella and I had married, she would only gain. But Ella's note convinced me in the end. It was in her hand, and the last phrase about smiling at her jewels and laughing at the world was certainly her own.

She charmed me as easily as she did the ogres. I never did discover why she hid after her father's wedding. She was probably avoiding a lovesick swain not wealthy enough or ancient enough to suit her. Her avoidance of me after the wedding was another trick, the meaning of which is too deep for me to fathom.

But her letters were the greatest deception of all. She seemed so good-hearted. But I suppose that's the way with such women: They wouldn't be minxes if they weren't masters of artifice and fraud. How she must have laughed when I confessed my faults to her!

There was more. In addition to minx, he called me flirt, harpy, siren, enchantress, temptress, and even monster. He ended by writing, "I wish I weren't in Ayortha. The silence here offers too much time for thought. A thousand times a day I swear never to think of her. At least I can promise never to write or speak of her again, and can force my pen and my voice to keep my word."

I endured six months of Hattie and Olive and Mum Olga by imagining my freedom when Lucinda released me from the curse.

I didn't give up writing to Char. Since the new letters

were never posted, I told him the truth about my life in Mum Olga's household. When Hattie told me that this earl or that duke loved her, I laughed over the absurdity of it to him. When Olive made me count her money again, he was informed.

"Every day she invents new hiding places for her wealth. There are coins in the hem of her gown, coins sewn into her sash, and coins buried in the stuffing of her waist roll. With all the metal concealed about her person, she had best not set foot on a boat."

When Mum Olga had me clean out the root cellar, and I found a tabby with her litter of kittens, Char learned of my delight. And when Mandy taught me cooking secrets, I shared them with him.

I also described my future without the curse.

"My first act," I wrote, "will be to confess that I love you. I'll beg pardon a thousand times for causing you unhappiness and make reparations by making you laugh a thousand times."

The night before Lucinda's reappearance, Hattie awakened me when she returned from a cotillion. She said I had to help her prepare for bed. I had never had to before, so I waited to learn her real reason.

"Tonight they talked of nothing but Prince Charmont's return next month," she began while I undressed her.

I knew exactly when he was coming home, so why was my heart beating so?

"They say that King Jerrold is going to hold three royal balls to welcome him. They say the prince will pick his wife at the balls. Ouch! Be careful."

I had stabbed her with a stay. For once, it was accidental.

"Mama says if I . . ."

I didn't hear anything more. Were the balls Char's idea? Did he really mean to find his bride there? Had he forgotten me? Could I make him remember when Lucinda freed me?

Hattie dismissed me eventually, and I spent the hours till dawn imagining my release from the curse and thinking about my reunion with Char. I couldn't decide whether I should steal one of Mum Olga's horses and ride to Ayortha to surprise him, or whether I should wait and amaze him at the balls.

In the morning I woke Mandy and tried to convince her to feign illness so she could call Lucinda immediately. But no, first we had to prepare Mum Olga's breakfast and wash all the dishes, and Mandy wouldn't use the smallest magic to speed the process.

When we were through at last, Mandy and I repaired to her bedroom, and I hid as before.

This time the room didn't fill with the scent of lilacs when Lucinda arrived. From my hiding place behind the curtains, I heard a rustling noise and then the sound of weeping.

"Stop sniveling," Mandy said.

The weeping became louder, more despairing. "I can't." The music and lilt were gone from Lucinda's voice. I heard panting as she fought to catch her breath. "But if I were still obedient," she puffed, "I would have to stop crying just because you told me to." More sobs. "What did I bring on those poor, innocent people? How could I have done big magic? And so carelessly!"

"Your gifts weren't a boon?" I'd never heard Mandy be sarcastic before.

"They were dreadful, terrible," Lucinda wailed.

I wondered if her experiences had been at all like mine.

"What happened?" Mandy asked, her voice kinder.

"It was much worse to be obedient, but being a squirrel was bad enough. Half the time I was cold and wet, and I was always hungry. I never got a decent night's sleep because I was too cramped, curling up in knotholes. Once, an eagle carried me off. I was only saved because it flew into a violent storm and dropped me over a tree."

"And when you were obedient?"

"I turned myself into the eight-year-old daughter of shopkeepers. I thought it was only fair to be a child, since I always bestowed obedience on infants. I suppose my parents meant well, but they insisted I eat the most awful food, and I had to go to bed before I was sleepy. My parents wouldn't let me disagree with them about anything. My father loved to read parables aloud, and I had to listen to every word. They commanded me to think about the morals, so even my thoughts had to be obedient.

"And all this I suffered at the hands of good people who loved me! If anything had happened to them, I shudder to think what would have become of me."

"You won't bestow any more gifts, then?"

"Never. I wish I could take them all back."

I stepped out from behind the curtain, even though I'd promised I wouldn't. "Please do take them back."

CHAPTER TWENTY-SIX

Lucinda gasped.

I gasped too. She wasn't Lucinda. Or was she? The enormous eyes were the same, but not the height. This fairy was stooped with age. And her perfect skin was wrinkled, with a mole next to her nose. I was seeing the real Lucinda, unshielded by magic.

"Mandy, who is this? You brought a human to spy on me!" She straightened for a moment, and I saw a hint of the young, beautiful Lucinda. Then she sighed. "You look familiar. Are you one of my victims?"

This was my chance, the chance for the freedom I always should have had, the chance to escape from my stepfamily, the chance to win Char back. But I was so nervous my voice was gone. I could only nod.

"What did I do to you, child?" she whispered, as though afraid of my answer.

I found my voice. "You made me obedient. Now you know how it is."

"I do, child."

She touched my cheek, and my heart rose.

"But I can't help you. I renounced big magic."

"Oh, Lady," I pleaded, "it would be a wondrous gift. I would be so grateful."

"Ella . . ." Mandy warned.

"Mandy, don't you think? Just this once." Lucinda shook her head, and wispy gray curls fluttered. "No, I mustn't. But if you ever have need of small magic, call on me. You have only to say the words, 'Lucinda, come to my aid.'" She kissed my forehead. "I remember you now. I thought you only spoke Ayorthaian."

I begged her. I told her about my circumstances. I wept. She wept with me—sobbed harder than I did—but stood firm. I pleaded with Mandy to persuade her, but Mandy refused.

"I can't, Lady," she said. "It was big magic to cast the spell in the first place. But it would be big magic to undo it too. Who can guess what would come of it?"

"Only good would come of it. Only good."

"I can't bear this," Lucinda wailed, wringing her hands dramatically. "I can't bear your distress. Farewell, child." She vanished.

I stormed out of Mandy's room and rushed to the library, where I could be alone, where no one was likely to make me scour anything or sew anything or say anything.

Now I couldn't go to the balls. Hattie and Olive would go with Mum Olga. They'd be free to dance with Char, and so would every other young lady in Frell. And some lass would win him over. His nature was loving, and he'd find someone to love.

As for me, I'd be lucky to glimpse him on the street. He wouldn't recognize me. My dirty servant's garb would rule out identification at a distance, and he'd never be close enough to see my face.

I could neither go to the balls nor escape from them. Hattie and Mum Olga talked of nothing else. Even Olive was interested to the extent of worrying about her gown.

"Sew it with gold thread," she instructed her maid. "Shouldn't I be as fine as Hattie?"

Shouldn't I be as fine as both of them? I cooked and scrubbed and waited on them in a fury. For two weeks I wouldn't speak to Mandy. The only sounds in the kitchen came from pots and pans as I slammed them down.

Then it came to me. Why couldn't I go? Char needn't know I was there. Everyone would be masked, at the beginning at least, although most would unmask quickly so he could admire their beauty. I never would. I'd see him, but he wouldn't see me.

Where was the harm, if he didn't recognize me? I decided to do it. I would fill my eyes with him. If I could approach him safely, I'd fill my ears. If anyone questioned me, I wouldn't be Ella; I'd invent a new name. I'd be content in his presence, nothing more.

I'd have to be careful of Hattie and Olive and Mum Olga. They probably wouldn't recognize me in a mask and an elegant gown, but I'd do well to keep away from them, especially from Hattie.

I made up with Mandy and told her my plan. She didn't comment on the risk I'd be taking, only asked, "Sweet, why go and break your heart again?"

My heart was still broken. I would see Char and it would mend. I'd leave him and it would break again. There were three balls. It would break three times.

I had grown tall enough to wear Mother's gowns. Mandy chose the best three and altered them in keeping with the current fashion, even adding a graceful train that would follow me everywhere. Small magic, she said.

She also found the mask I'd worn at Father's wedding, white with tiny white beads along its edges.

In the days preceding the ball, if there were moments when Char and the balls weren't in my mind, they were when I was asleep. Awake, I'd picture myself, radiantly beautiful, mounting the palace steps. I'd be late and the whole court would be there already. An old servant would mutter, "At last, a damsel worthy of our prince." People would turn to stare, and a sigh, of envy or appreciation, would rustle through the assembly. Char would hurry to . . .

I wouldn't allow him to see me. The old servant might approve me, but I would slip in unnoticed by anyone else. Within, noblemen in my proximity would beg me to dance. I'd oblige them, and the steps would carry me near Char. He'd see me and wonder who I was. After the dance, he'd attempt to find me, but I'd elude him. The next time he'd see me, I'd be in the arms of another partner. I'd smile at the stranger, and Char's heart would be touched. He'd . . .

My thoughts were nonsense. I would see Char and be invisible to him. Perhaps I'd see him fall in love with another maiden.

At night, I searched my magic book for illustrations of Char or anything written by him. But the book fell open to pages written in Ayorthaian—written by Areida in her diary. I read eagerly.

She wrote,

The inn has never had such important guests before. Prince Charmont and his knights stayed here last night! Mother was so nervous, she backed into the trestle table while curtsying. It went over, and Aunt Eneppe's vase smashed into a hundred pieces. Mother, Father, I, Ollo, Uflimu, Isti, and even Ettime went down on our knees, picking up shards so the prince wouldn't step on something sharp. It was so crowded on the floor, I bumped into someone's shoulder. When I turned to apologize, I was face-to-face with the prince, who was crawling about with the rest of us!

He insisted on paying for the vase. He said it never would have happened if not for him. Then he apologized for knocking into me! I couldn't answer him. No words would come. I could only nod and smile and hope I didn't seem too much of a bumpkin.

At dinner, when I brought his ale, I did manage to speak, perhaps because I truly had a question, not simply a wish to impress. I told him I'd been at finishing school when Ella ran away, and I asked if he knew whether she was safe.

When I said her name, one of the knights called out, "The ogre tamer. What ever happened to her?"

The prince was quiet for so long after my question that I worried I'd offended him. But when he spoke, he didn't seem angry.

"You were her friend?" he asked. "You liked her?"

I told him Ella was the best friend I ever had. He paused again, and I feared he would say she had died. But he finally answered that he believed her to be well and married to a rich gentleman. He added, "She is happy, I think. She is rich, so she is happy."

Without thinking, I blurted, "Ella doesn't care about riches." Then I realized I'd contradicted a prince!

"How do you know?" he said.

I answered, "At school everyone hated me because I wasn't wealthy and because I spoke with an accent. She was the only one who was kind."

"Perhaps she's changed," he said.

"I don't think so, your Highness." I contradicted him twice!

That was the end of our conversation, and I shall remember it forever. I watched him all evening, before and after we talked. Before, he had talked and joked with his men. After, he spoke no more.

Married! How could it be? I wish I could see her again.

I wished I could see Areida. I wished I could have seen Char's face when she defended me, but no illustrations accompanied her journal.

December 12, the day of the first ball, dawned clear and mild, but by noon clouds had gathered and the wind had become sharp and cold.

My gowns hung in Mandy's wardrobe. The glass slippers Char and I had found were safely buried at the bottom of my carpetbag. Since they'd be hidden under my petticoats, there was little likelihood that Char would see and identify them.

Hattie's preparations began after breakfast and continued endlessly.

"It's not tight enough, Ella. Pull harder."

"Will that do?" My fingers were striped red and white from tugging at her laces. If she could still breathe, I wasn't to blame.

"Let me see." She curtsied at herself in the mirror

and rose, panting and smiling. "I shall be desolate if you don't remember me, Prince," she cooed at her reflection. Then she spoke over her shoulder. "Am I not magnificent, Ella? Don't you wish you could look as I do and go to the ball?"

"Magnificent, ravishing. Yes, I wish I could." Anything to make her go.

"Pearls would set my hair off to advantage. Fetch them, there's a good girl."

Two hours later, after Mum Olga called her three times and threatened to leave without her, she declared herself perfect and departed.

At last I was free to bathe and dress. Instead of the kitchen soap I usually used, I helped myself to Hattie's store of bath oils and fragrant soaps. Mandy produced a fleecy towel and a fine scrub brush.

"Tonight I'll be your lady-in-waiting," she said, pouring steaming water into the tub.

When your servant is your fairy godmother, you're never scalded, and your water never gets cold. You become sparkling clean, but the water never gets dirty.

I soaked away a year of cinders and grime and Mum Olga's orders and Hattie's edicts and Olive's demands. When I rose from the bath and stepped into the robe Mandy held for me, I was no longer a scullery maid but the equal of anyone at Char's ball.

My gown was a spring green embroidered with leaves of darker green and plump yellow buds. Mandy had done her work well. In accordance with the latest fashion, my waist tapered to a narrow point, and my train trailed two feet behind me. In the glass, I saw Mandy curtsy.

"You're lovely, Lady." She seemed close to tears. I hugged her. She squeezed me tight, and I inhaled the sweet smell of freshly baked bread.

I turned back to the glass and raised my mask, which covered most of my forehead and half of my cheeks, with small holes for my eyes. With half my head hidden, my mouth appeared strange and unknown even to me. The transformation was thorough. With the mask, I was not Ella.

Nor was I perfectly dressed. I had no jewels. My throat was unfashionably bare. But it would have to do. I didn't have to be the most elegant creature at the ball; I only had to see Char.

When I ran down to our front door, I discovered that icy rain was falling in sheets. If I walked the quarter mile to the castle, I would be soaked. I could go to the ball without jewels, but not wet through and shivering.

"Mandy! What can I do?"

"Oh, sweet. You can stay home."

I knew there would be two more balls, and that it probably wouldn't sleet tomorrow. But it might, and I had set my heart on going tonight.

"Isn't there some small magic—a fairy umbrella, something—that would keep me dry?"

"No, love. Not small magic."

The weather was such a stupid thing to separate me from Char. Mandy hadn't made the rain, but she could have ended it.

"I wish you were a *real* fairy, one who wasn't afraid to do anything." I had a mad idea and acted on it without considering its wisdom. I said the words Lucinda had taught me, "Lucinda, come to my aid." If anyone would think keeping me dry wasn't big magic, that one would be Lucinda.

"Ella!" Mandy protested. "Don't—"

The order came too late. Lucinda appeared between us.

She still looked old, but she stood straighter than the last time I'd seen her, and many of her wrinkles had disappeared.

"Ahhh. Sweet child. You need my help." She smiled, and the young Lucinda shone through. "So long as it's not too big, I shall do what I can."

I explained.

"Going to a ball? Like that? No, it won't do." She touched my neck, and it was hung so heavy with jewels that it took all my finishing school training to keep my head up.

Mandy snorted.

"Perhaps it's too much for small magic," Lucinda agreed. The weight vanished, replaced by a thin silver chain from which hung a white lily made of the same kind of glass as my slippers. I felt a slight pressure on my head, and lifted off a tiara fashioned as a garland of the same flowers.

"It's beautiful."

Lucinda replaced it on my hair. "Now, you need a coach. That shouldn't be too troublesome."

"How can you call a coach small magic?" Mandy demanded. "And horses, and a coachman, and footmen. People and animals! You've forgotten your lesson."

"No, I haven't. I won't shape them from the air. I'll form them out of real things. That should satisfy your scruples, Mandy dear."

Mandy grunted, which I knew was not agreement, but Lucinda continued gaily.

"Earlier this evening in Frell I spied a giant's cart filled with pumpkins. An orange coach will be splendid."

A rumbling noise reached us. Outside, a mass, darker than the storm, took shape and grew larger. A seven-foot-high pumpkin rolled toward us and came to rest in the street outside the manor.

I watched Lucinda. She muttered no incantations, waved no wand. For a moment, her gaze shifted, and she seemed to stare within, not out. Then she winked at me.

"Look, child."

The pumpkin had been transformed into a gleaming coach with brass door handles and windows through which lacy curtains peeked.

"Mice will make plump horses," she said.

Six fat brown mice raced across the tiles of the hall. They vanished, and six horses appeared before the coach. A white rat became the coachman, and six lizards were transformed into footmen.

"They're wonderful!" I said. "Thank you."

She beamed.

Mandy glowered. "Anything can happen, you idiot!"

"What can happen? I'll make it safer. Ella, child, you'll have to leave the ball early. At midnight, your coach will become a pumpkin again, and the animals will regain their original shape until your next ball. The tiara and necklace will disappear."

I would have only three hours with Char. They would have to be enough.

"Ah, how glorious to be young and going to a ball." Lucinda vanished.

Glorious! Yes, to see Char. Nothing more. "Goodbye, Mandy," I said.

"Wait!" She ran to the kitchen.

I stood impatiently and gazed outside. As I watched, an orange carpet unfurled itself and rolled from the coach's door to ours. If I waited much longer, it would be wet and useless.

Mandy returned with her umbrella, uncompromisingly black and with two bent spokes.

"Here, love. I hope you won't be sorry. I won't hug you and muss your dress." She kissed me. "Go now."

I stepped onto the carpet and raised the umbrella. The coachman jumped down from his perch and opened the carriage door.

CHAPTER TWENTY-SEVEN

A few guests were still arriving when my carriage reached the castle. Before I emerged, I made certain my mask was securely tied.

I had been here before, as a week-old infant brought to meet my sovereign, but not since. The hall was twice as tall as Mum Olga's. Every wall was covered with tapestries: hunting scenes, court scenes, pastoral scenes. Along the walls to my right and to my left a line of marble pillars marched to the end of the hall. I tried not to gape. Soon I'd be counting windows.

"Mistress . . ." A young squire offered me a glass of wine. It was delightful not to be a servant. "The prince is greeting his guests. There is the queue." He waved at a file of courtiers, mostly women, that wound from the huge double doors to the prince, a small figure at the far reach of the hall. Most of the women had already unmasked, so Char would be sure to see their lovely eyes or classical noses.

The squire added, "They're each scheming to make the prince propose marriage on the spot." He bowed. "Dance with me, Lady. The line will wait."

An order. A group of musicians played near the prince, and perhaps a dozen guests danced.

"With pleasure," I said, pitching my voice a tone lower than usual.

My eyes kept straying from my partner. Char smiled at each guest, bowed, nodded, spoke. Once he laughed. Making him laugh had been my domain. The damsel who caused the laughter was of middle height, slender, with blond, wavy hair cascading to her waist. She had removed her mask, but her back was turned, so I couldn't see her face.

Hattie and Olive and Mum Olga weren't in line. They were probably off eating somewhere, but Hattie would certainly return soon. She wouldn't leave a room for long while Char occupied it.

My dance ended as the clock struck the quarter before ten.

"Thank you," I said.

"No squire can hold a lady's attention tonight." He left me.

Just over two hours remained. I retired to a chair at the edge of the hall, as close to Char as I dared.

Three gentlemen asked me to dance, but I declined each invitation. I became simply a pair of eyes, staring through my mask at Char. I needed no ears because I was too far off to hear his voice, no words because I was too distant for speech, and no thoughts—those I saved for later.

He bent his head. I loved the hairs on the nape of his neck. He moved his lips. I admired their changing shape. He clasped a hand. I blessed his fingers.

Once, the power of my gaze drew his eyes. I looked away quickly and noticed Hattie, hovering a few feet beyond the line, her lips clenched in a fawning smile.

He spoke to the last guest. Last but one. My resolution to be unseen gave way. The last in line would be me. I rose and hurried to reach him before Hattie could pounce.

I curtsied. He bowed. When we both straightened, I found I had grown closer to his height.

"What is your name, Lady?" He smiled politely.

I found my voice with difficulty. "Lela."

We were silent.

"Do you live here in Frell, Lady Lela?"

"In Bast, Highness." I named a town near the elves' Forest.

He looked past me, ready to move on. "I hope you enjoy the ball and your stay in Frell."

I couldn't let him go. "Abensa ohudo. Isseni imi essete urebu amouffa." I spoke with a heavy Kyrrian accent.

"You speak Ayorthaian!" His attention was captured.

"Not well. My uncle was born there. He's a singer. His voice can charm wood."

Char's smile was genuine now. "I miss their songs. I was glad to leave, but now I miss everything."

I hummed a stanza of Areida's favorite song, a sad one, about a farmer whose family is starving. Char joined me, singing softly. Near us, heads turned. I saw Hattie frown with her smile still frozen in place.

When we finished, he bowed again. "Would you favor me with a dance?"

Over all the others I was his choice! I curtsied, and he took my hand.

Our hands knew each other. Char looked at me, startled. "Have we met before, Lady?"

"I've never left Bast, but I've longed to see Frell my whole life."

He nodded.

The clock struck eleven.

The dance was a gavotte, too spirited for talk. Rapid movement was a relief in the midst of so much feeling. We flew through the hall, perfectly in step. Char smiled at me. I smiled back, happy.

We separated. I twined arms with a succession of momentary partners—dukes, earls, knights, squires—and back to Char. A final whirl, and the dance ended.

"I love a gavotte," I said, touching to make sure my mask was still properly in place. "The rush, the sweep, the whoosh!" What nonsense was I talking?

"It's the same with stair rails, the same feeling," he said. "Do you like to slide?" His voice was eager.

Stair rails! Did he suspect me? I forced a sigh. "No, Majesty. I'm terrified of heights."

"Oh." His polite tone had returned.

"Do you?"

"Do I what?"

"Like to slide down stair rails?"

"Oh, yes. I used to."

"I wish I could enjoy it. This fear of heights is an affliction."

He nodded, a show of sympathy but not much interest. I was losing him.

"Especially," I added, "as I've grown taller."

He stared. Then he laughed in surprised delight. I was a fool for behaving so much like myself. The clock struck the half hour.

Char started. "Half after eleven! I've neglected my

guests." He became the courteous host again. "Refreshments are in the next room, if you care to partake of them." He waved at an archway. Then, "I'll look for you later."

He hoped to see me again! Lela, that is.

I hurried out of the hall. Outside, the sleet had stopped. The pumpkin coach glistened in a line of black carriages. I climbed in. When we arrived at home, the coachman handed me out, remounted, and flicked his whip. The horses started off.

In the morning Hattie told me about her share in the ball, bidding me to sit on a low stool while the family ate their breakfast.

"He danced with me," Hattie said, her teeth stained purple from a blueberry muffin. "And only good manners prevented him from spending the rest of the evening at my side."

"When will you pay me?" Olive asked.

"Must I pay? Aren't you glad you danced with the prince?"

"You said you'd give me three coins for every time he couldn't dance with anyone else because of me. You owe me . . ." She thought. "Eight coins."

"How many times did he dance with you?" I asked.

"Three times. I asked him four times, but the last time he said he had to see to his other guests."

I vowed not to approach Char during the second ball. It was too dangerous.

The evening was clear, but Lucinda provided the coach anyway. My tiara and pendant were pink roses.

My gown was a silvery blue with a pale purple petticoat.

Tonight there was no receiving line. I searched for a seat where I'd have a clear view of the dance and where others would have a poor view of me. I found one in a recess partially blocked by a giant fern in a stone pot.

I scrutinized Char's dancing partners, although I knew I had no right to resent a rival. He danced three times with the yellow-haired wench who'd made him laugh the night before. She wore no mask and was lovely. I couldn't leave him to her.

The clock struck the half hour. Soon it would be eleven. I checked my mask, then left my hiding place and stood with the others who observed the dance.

Char saw me. Over the shoulder of his partner, he mouthed, "Wait for me."

I grew roots. An earthquake could not have moved me. The clock struck a quarter before eleven. It struck eleven. If it had struck the end of the world, I'd have stayed as I was.

The final figure ended, and he came to me.

"Will you dance?" he asked. "I looked for you."

Did I have time? I accepted his arm, and we stepped into the dance, a slow sarabande.

"I was here all the while. I watched you."

"What did you see?"

"An excellent host who had little real enjoyment in the ball." Except when he danced with the blond beauty.

"Was it so apparent?"

"It was to me."

He changed the subject. "Will you be here tomorrow? My father has asked me to perform an Ayorthaian song."

"When will you sing?" Before midnight, please.

"Sometime late." He grinned. "If I'm lucky, many of my guests will have gone. They needn't all hear their future ruler disgrace himself."

"There will be no disgrace, not if you were taught in Ayortha. What will you sing?"

"A homecoming song." He sang in my ear.

"Oak, granite,
Lilies by the road,
Remember me?
I remember you.
Clouds brushing
Clover hills,
Remember me?
Sister, child,
Grown tall,
Remember me?
I remember you."

The dance ended, and he stopped. "There's more. I want you to hear it. Will you?"

I resolved to stay late the next night. I'd manage to reach home without Lucinda's gifts, even if I had to swim. "I'll be delighted to, but I must leave now tonight. I'm expected by twelve." How close to midnight was it now? He would think it odd if my jewelry vanished!

"Oh. I'd hoped . . . I'm sorry. I mustn't . . ." He bowed.

I curtsied. "Till tomorrow, Majesty."

"One last thing." He caught my hand. "Please call me Char."

CHAPTER TWENTY-EIGHT

I rode home, calling myself a dolt but rejoicing nonetheless. In my room I opened my magic book to see if it would show me anything about the ball or Char's thoughts. There was nothing. The next morning I tried again and found an entry in his journal from the night before.

How dare she! That fright—Hattie—rushed at me the instant Lela left. "Some wenches will stoop to anything to intrigue a man," she said. "I should be devastated if I had to wear a mask in order to be interesting."

She warned me the mask might conceal anything: a deformity, advancing age, the face of a known bandit. "If I were sovereign," she said, "I would order her to remove her mask."

I wanted to reply, "If you were sovereign, every Kyrrian would wish you'd don one."

Certainly I've wondered why Lela hides her face, but it may be the custom in Bast. If she is a bandit, she's courageous to come to court. More likely she is *disfigured. Maybe she's has a scar, or one eyelid droops, or her nose is a mottled purple.*

I don't care. I'm pleased to have found a friend at these balls, where I expected to find only tedium.

Does ~~Ella~~ Lela want more than friendship? Why did I write that name?

Did she come to these balls, as every other maiden did, hoping to wed a prince? (No matter what I am like, so long as I am a prince.)

I confess: I do wish to see her face.

I turned the page and found a reckoning from Olive to Hattie.

You o me 6 KJs. I danced with him to times wen you wer eeting. Pa me.

In the afternoon, I slipped out of the manor to the greenhouse near the menagerie. There I picked daisies and wove the flowers into a garland to replace Lucinda's tiara. If I was to stay at the ball after midnight, I couldn't wear Lucinda's jewels.

My gown for the last ball was my favorite: white, with a low neckline edged in lace. The skirt parted in front to reveal a petticoat with three lace flounces. In back, my skirt was tied with a large bow that flowed into the graceful sweep of my train.

I faced myself in the mirror and began to set the garland in my hair, but Mandy stopped me.

"Here's something better, love." She handed me two packages wrapped in tissue paper. "Open them."

They were a tiara of woven silver leaves and a silver chain on which hung an aster made of lapis.

"Oh, Mandy!"

"I bought them at the market. They won't disappear at midnight." She placed the tiara on my hair and fastened the chain around my neck. "You make them beautiful, sweet."

I looked in the mirror. Mandy's selections added something that Lucinda's creations hadn't—just right for my gown and just right for me.

Char was waiting for me at the palace entrance. When the carriage drove up, he dashed to help me out before the coachman could step down. The clock struck half after eight. The beginning of the last ball.

"You look splendid," he said, bowing.

I was touched by his gallantry, since he believed me disfigured.

As we went inside he said, "Your carriage is an unusual color."

"Not in Bast." If he knew much about Bast, I was in for trouble—unless orange coaches *were* common there.

He took my arm. "May I visit you there?"

"Bast would be honored."

"And you?"

"I'd be honored too."

"If I'm going to visit your family, you should meet mine."

"I'll be delighted, someday."

"Now is a good time. They're nearby; you're nearby."

"Now? King Jerrold?"

He chuckled. "That's who my father is."

"But . . ."

"He's kind to everyone except ogres. You needn't worry."

The king rose when we entered. I curtsied, blushing for my rudeness in wearing a mask before him. When I rose, he was beaming at Char. Queen Daria was smiling too.

I'd seen them many times, but never so close. The queen had a wide face, perfect for broad smiles. An honest face. Char resembled his father, but softened a bit. The king's face was severe in repose, although merry now.

"Mother, Father, may I introduce Lady Lela, my new friend and acquaintance from Bast, where the carriages are orange."

"Lady Lela." King Jerrold took my hand. He had the roundest, deepest voice I'd ever heard. "Welcome to Frell."

"Most welcome." Queen Daria embraced me. "I've waited long to meet the maiden my son loves."

"I don't love her, Mother. That is, I like her, certainly."

Over the queen's shoulder, I saw Char looking silly with embarrassment.

Queen Daria held me away from her and searched my face. "I can't tell through the mask, but you remind me of a lady I admired. She had the most playful spirit I ever knew." She added so only I could hear, "If you are like her, then Char has chosen well."

She released me, and I stepped away, dazed. I was certain she had meant Mother.

"Lady Lela is proof I haven't been polite and distant to everyone," Char said.

"Excellent proof," King Jerrold answered. "Bring along more proof and we'll be convinced." He frowned at my mask.

"We should return to my guests," Char said hastily.

As we left, I heard Queen Daria say, "I don't remember any orange coaches in Bast."

Back in the hall, Char asked me to save a dance for him later. "Just now, I'd better be polite and distant some more."

I didn't want him to go. Every instant of our final evening was too precious to lose even one. But I nodded, and he left me. I watched the dance and turned down partners.

"Mistress . . ." Hattie stood before me, simpering. "I've wanted to catch you alone, my dear. I am Lady Hattie, daughter of Dame Olga."

Lela had no reason to hate Hattie. "I'm happy to meet another Frellan."

"Charmont says you live in Bast."

No one called him Charmont.

She proceeded to pump me about my family and circumstances, pressing me until I said, "I hadn't thought it was the custom here to interrogate visitors."

"I apologize, but one has to be so careful when one is connected to royalty. You see, Charmont and I have an understanding. We are secretly engaged."

Had she gone mad, to speak such a falsehood?

"To protect him, I must ask you to remove your mask. I must see what lies beneath."

Thank heavens she had asked and not ordered. "You may ask, but I shall not oblige. Good evening, Lady Hattie." I turned and began to walk away.

"Lela, there you are!"

Char was back. "Now dance with me," he said. "Your

prince commands you to. I want to spend the rest of the ball with you." He bowed to Hattie, standing a few feet away. "Excuse us."

I curtsied, reveling in her fury.

"They are all asking about you," he said, pulling me close as the dance required. "'Who is this mysterious stranger?' they say."

"The maiden who wears a mask."

"Why . . ." He stopped himself and changed subjects, speaking of court affairs.

I wondered how many more dances we'd have. The clock chimed half after nine. In a few hours Lela would be gone forever. I'd never be so close to Char again.

Despite a fierce struggle, I began to cry. He might not have seen because of the mask, but a tear coursed down my cheek.

"Lela. I'm so sorry!" There was so much remorse in his voice that I was startled.

"Why? What were you saying? I'm the one to apologize. I wasn't listening. I was thinking how sad I'll be to leave Frell." I laughed a little. "No more balls every night."

"But you can come back, can't you?"

"I suppose. But it won't be the same. You can never go back to a moment when you were happy."

"That's true." The dance ended. "Would you like to go outside? Every time the musicians start up, I'm reminded of all the maidens with whom I should be dancing."

Outdoors we strolled through the castle gardens while I kept listening for chimes. How much time had passed? How much was left?

Char spoke of Frell, asking whether I'd visited this sight or that, and describing each one for me. I must have answered him reasonably when I had to. But if called upon to repeat what I said or what he said, I couldn't. Most of my mind and all of my heart were set on the sound of his voice, the warmth of his arm in mine, the rhythm of our steps together, the fresh scent of the night air. And on the wish that each minute would last a year. I cried again, but in the dark he didn't see. And the clock moved relentlessly on: ten, half after, eleven, half after.

"That's enough," he said finally. "I can face them now."

Inside we danced again. "Soon it will be time for me to sing. After that, I'll either be surrounded by worshiping music lovers or be shunned by all."

"Surrounded," I said. "And I would never shun you."

"I wonder. You may shun me if you know the truth." He took a breath and was suddenly quite formal. "I apologize if I unintentionally raised your expectations, but I've resolved never to marry."

So the balls hadn't been his idea. I stifled a triumphant laugh. "You didn't mislead me. I've only been saving stories for home. I'll tell them, 'The prince said thus-and-so to me, and I said thus-and-so back to him. And, Mother, I made him laugh. I made our prince laugh. And Father, he danced with me—one night with almost no one except me.' 'What did he wear?' my sister will want to know. 'Did he have his sword with him always?' Father will ask."

Char tightened his hold on my waist. "Marriage is

supposed to be forever, but friendship can be forever too. Will you . . ."

I felt something at the back of my head. Hattie, dancing nearby with the Earl of Demby, snatched off my mask. I let go of Char and covered my face with my hands, but not quickly enough.

CHAPTER TWENTY-NINE

"Ella!" Hattie shrieked.

Char gasped. "Ella?"

I broke away from him and began to run as the clock struck midnight. Char would have caught me in a moment, but Hattie must have held him somehow.

Outside, a huge pumpkin stood uselessly in the line of carriages. I continued to flee. A white rat skittered across my path. Somewhere I lost one of my slippers. I ran on, listening for pursuers.

At home, maybe Mandy would know what to do. Or I'd hide in the cellar, in the stable—somewhere. How could I have gone to the balls? To put Char and Kyrria in such danger!

"Mandy!" I shouted as soon as I reached the manor. A servant stared at me. I ran into the kitchen. "I've endangered Char again, and Kyrria! What can I do?"

"Pack your things," Mandy said as soon as she understood my rushed explanation.

"Where shall I go?"

"I'll come with you. We'll find work as cooks. Hurry."

"Can't you pack for us by magic?" She'd done it before. It was just small magic.

"Nothing is small magic in a moment like this. Go!"

Fairies! I raced to my room and began to throw things into my carpetbag. I had little; it would be the work of a minute. I heard the door open downstairs. There were voices. We'd never manage to leave. I tore off my ball gown and donned my tattered servant's wear, rubbing the sooty skirt across my face. Over my hair I tied a ragged length of linen.

Nancy appeared at my door. "It's the prince! He wants to see everyone."

I didn't move.

She giggled nervously. "He won't eat us, at least I hope not. Come."

I followed her, my heart drumming loud enough to drown out all thought.

He stood in the hall with his knights and our entire household. In the midst of all that was more important, I hated him to see me covered in rags and cinders.

I stationed myself behind the tallest manservant, but Char and the knights walked among us. Straining for a new disguise of servant and simpleton, I sucked on my fist and stared about vacantly.

Sir Stephan found me. "Here's a maid," he said. "Come, lass." He took my hand and pulled me to Char.

"Ella! Ella? Why are you dressed so?"

"Your Majesty, I'm . . ." I was about to deny my name, but Hattie spoke for me.

"That's only Cinders, the scullery maid," she said. "Sire, would you care for a refreshment now you're here?"

"She's a scullery maid?"

"A scullery maid. Of no account. But our cook, Mandy, has cakes fit for a prince."

The door wasn't far. Sir Stephan still held my hand. I pulled, but couldn't break away.

"Lass," Char said to me. "I won't hurt you, no matter what." He cupped his hand under my chin and tilted my face up to his. I wanted to catch his hand and kiss it.

As soon as we touched, I knew he recognized me. He brought my slipper out from his cloak. "It belonged to Ella, and will fit her alone, whether she is a scullery maid or a duchess."

A chair was brought. I wished for normal-sized feet.

"That's my slipper," Hattie said. "It's been missing for years."

"Your feet are too big," Olive blurted.

"Try it," Char told Hattie.

"I lost it because it kept falling off." She sat and removed her own slipper. I caught the familiar smell of her feet. She couldn't wedge her toes in.

"I'm younger than Hattie," Olive said. "So my feet are smaller. Probably."

They were bigger.

Now it was my turn. Char knelt, holding the slipper. I extended my foot and he guided it. The slipper fit perfectly, of course. What was I going to do?

His face was close to mine. He must have seen my terror. "You needn't be Ella if you don't want to be," he said softly.

He was so good.

"I'm not," I said. But in spite of myself, tears streamed down my cheeks.

I saw hope spread across his face. "That letter was rubbish. A trick." He glared at Hattie, then turned to me, his look probing. "Do you love me?" He still spoke softly. "Tell me."

An order. "I do." I was sobbing and smiling at once. How was I going to give him up again?

Char was jubilant. His voice rang out. "Then marry me!"

Another order. I nodded and continued to weep. But my hand found its way into his.

"Don't marry him, Ella," Hattie commanded, giving my name away for once and all.

I withdrew my hand. "I can't," I said. Perhaps Hattie would save us.

"Hattie, don't be a fool," Mum Olga snapped. "Don't you want to be stepsister to the queen and make her give you whatever you like?" She smiled at me. "His Highness is kind enough to want to marry you, Ella, my sweet."

It had begun. The curse would make Hattie and Mum Olga as grand as they wanted to be, and it would provide endless wealth for Olive.

Char was looking at me with such gladness, and I loved him so. I was the cause of his joy and would be the cause of his destruction: a secret delivered to his enemies, a letter written in my own hand, a covert signal given by me, poison in his glass, a dagger in his ribs, a fall from a parapet.

"Marry me, Ella," he said again, the order a whisper now. "Say you'll marry me."

Anyone else could have said no or yes. This wasn't a royal command. Char probably had no idea he'd given an order.

But I had to obey—wanted to obey—hated to harm him—wanted to marry him. I would destroy my love and my land. They were in danger, and no one could rescue them. We were all doomed, all cursed.

Char was too precious to hurt, too precious to lose, too precious to betray, too precious to marry, too precious to kill, too precious to obey.

Words rose in me, filled my mouth, pushed against my lips. Yes, I'll marry you. Yes, I love you. Yes! Yes! Yes!

I swallowed, forcing them down, but they tore at my throat. A strangled noise erupted from me, but not words, not consent.

He put a hand on my shoulder. I must have frightened him, but I couldn't see his face; my vision had turned inward where the battle raged. I heard Lucinda's voice, "My gift to Ella is obedience. She will always be obedient." I saw Mandy telling me to eat my birthday cake. I saw SEEf leering at me and heard him. "No need to be persuasive with this one. It'd cook itself if we told it to." I saw Olive counting my coins, Mum Olga standing over me while I scrubbed the courtyard, Hattie wearing Mother's necklace.

I'd eaten the cake, drunk the Tonic, given up the necklace, slaved for my stepmother, let Olive suck me dry. They'd gotten all they wanted of me, but they weren't going to get Char. Never. Never.

Be obedient. Marry him. Say yes. Say yes. Say yes.

The tears streaming from my eyes were acid, burning my cheeks. My mouth filled with liquid, bile and blood from biting my tongue, salty and corrosive and sweet.

In spite of myself my mouth opened. Consent had won. Obedience had won.

But I clamped my hand over my mouth. My yes was stillborn.

I remembered Char at Mother's funeral, waiting for me while I wept, grieving for Mother too. I heard his promise at the menagerie. "And soon I shall catch a centaur and give it to you." I saw him binding SEEF's ankles. I saw him, buttonless doublet flapping, bow to Father after we'd flown down the stair rails. I saw the ball and King Jerrold beaming at his son, the hope and future of Kyrria.

Say yes and be happy. Say yes and live. Obey. Marry him.

I began to rock in my chair. Forward, the words were about to come. Back, I reeled them in. Faster and faster. The legs of the chair thudded on the tiles and pounded in my ears. Marry him. I won't. Marry him. I won't.

Then I lost sense of all of it. I went on rocking and crying, but my thought burrowed within, concentrated in a point deep in my chest, where there was room for only one truth: I must save Char. For a moment I rested inside myself, safe, secure, certain, gaining strength. In that moment I found a power beyond any I'd had before, a will and a determination I would never have needed if not for Lucinda, a fortitude I hadn't been able to find for a lesser cause. And I found my voice.

"No," I shouted. "I won't marry you. I won't do it. No one can force me!" I swallowed and wiped my mouth on my filthy sleeve. I leaped up, ready to defy anyone.

"Who would force you?" Char sounded shocked.

"No matter who. I won't, I won't. They can't make me, no one can make me. I won't marry you."

Olive said, "She'll marry you. You told her to. She has to listen." She laughed. "Marry him and give me your money."

"I won't! Stop ordering me to!" I was still shouting, invigorated. I wanted to march, waving banners. Char would not die because of me. Char would live. Live and prosper.

"She doesn't have to marry me," he said.

"Hush, Olive," Hattie said. "Ella, go to your room. His Majesty can have no further need of you."

Char said, "I have great need of her."

"Hush, Hattie!" I said, intoxicated with my success. "I don't want to go to my room. Everyone must know I shan't marry the prince." I ran to the door to our street, opened it, and called out into the night, "I shan't marry the prince." I turned back into the hall and ran to Char and threw my arms about his neck. "I shan't marry you." I kissed his cheek. He was safe from me.

He turned my head and kissed me on the mouth. The kiss swept through me, and I clung to him, trembling.

From behind me, Hattie shrilled, "Go to your room this instant. I command you."

I ignored her, but Char pulled away.

"Why won't you marry me? Why not, if you love me?"

"I'm cursed. You wouldn't be safe if I were your wife." What was I saying? I hadn't told anyone about the curse since I was eight. Mother had forbidden it. Had someone told me to?

No one had. Then why . . .

My thoughts wouldn't settle.

I wasn't going to marry Char, that was certain. He looked so handsome, smiling from our kiss, then frowning in confusion, a smudge of my soot on his nose. I wiped it off. Saving him made him more mine than ever.

Could my refusal mean the spell was broken? Could it? I took stock of myself. I did feel different: larger, fuller, more complete, no longer divided against myself—compulsion to comply against wish to refuse. Larger, but lighter, much lighter—a burden shed. A massive burden.

I'd defied Olive's command as well as Char's. And Hattie had sent me to my room, but I was still here. I had told my secret, but I felt no dizziness, no pain.

"You're free. The curse is over, love." Mandy was at my side, hugging me. "You rescued yourself when you rescued the prince. I'm that proud and glad, sweet, I could shout."

I had been able to break the curse myself. I'd had to have reason enough, love enough to do it, to find the will and the strength. My safety from the ogres hadn't been enough; zhulpH's rescue hadn't been enough, especially not with guards about; my slavery to Mum Olga hadn't been enough. Kyrria was enough. Char was enough.

Now it was over. Ended forever. I was made anew. Ella. Just Ella. Not Ella, the slave. Not a scullery maid. Not Lela. Not Eleanor. Ella. Myself unto myself. One. Me.

I tore off the rag that covered my hair. Then I curtsied to Char.

"When you asked for my hand a few minutes ago, I

was still too young to marry." I looked up at him and saw a smile start. "I'm older now, so much older that not only can I marry, but I can beg you to marry me." I knelt and took his hand.

He didn't let me kneel before him. He pulled me up and kissed me again. I took that to signify his consent.

In a month we married. For the ceremony I wore my first new gown in a year and Mother's necklace, which I reclaimed from Hattie. After my deception had been explained to them, King Jerrold and Queen Daria welcomed me joyously into the royal family.

My stepfamily was not invited to the wedding and had to celebrate, if they wished, in the streets with the rest of Frell. Father was invited, but he was traveling and didn't receive the invitation until it was too late.

Areida did attend. We renewed our friendship and swore to visit each other often, an oath we've kept faithfully.

All the exotic peoples, except ogres, were represented at the ceremony. Slannen gave us a new pottery piece by Agulen, an elf child embracing a tree. zhatapH and zhulpH were there, zhulpH still a toddler, since gnomes grow more slowly than humans. Uaaxee came too and was responsible for keeping our animal guest, Apple, from galloping the length of the palace hall.

Although we didn't invite Lucinda, she arrived anyway—with a gift.

"No need," Char and I chimed together.

"Remember when you were a squirrel," Mandy said.

But the gift was what Father would have called a fairy trifle. It was a box, no larger than my thumbnail, which grew or shrank to accommodate whatever it was called upon to hold. Wonderfully useful and not harmful at all. We thanked Lucinda enthusiastically until she glowed with pleasure.

In time Hattie became reconciled to our marriage and used her connection to us to her best advantage. She never married, but Olive did. A garrulous widower fell in love with her unwavering attention. When she'd demand that he talk to her, he'd tell her about his triumphs, his enemies, his opinions on everything. She wasn't anxious to wed; in exchange for her consent, he paid her twenty KJs every day and served a white cake with every meal.

Father and Mum Olga continued to love at a distance. After my marriage, he became successful again, trading on the respect commanded by the royal family. Char watched over him and intervened when necessary to save him or his victims from the consequences of his chicanery.

Mandy lived with us as cook and godmother of our children—and secret performer of small magic to protect us from colds, broken crockery, and the sundry inconveniences of a royal household. Nancy lived at the palace too, and commanded a legion of servants, several of whom were in charge of polishing stair rails for their sliding monarchs.

I refused to become a princess but adopted the titles of Court Linguist and Cook's Helper. I also refused to stay at home when Char traveled, and learned every language and dialect that came our way. When we left the children behind, my magic book kept us informed of their doings.

Decisions were a delight after the curse. I loved having the power to say yes or no, and refusing anything was a special pleasure. My contrariness kept Char laughing, and his goodness kept me in love.

And so, with laughter and love, we lived happily ever after.

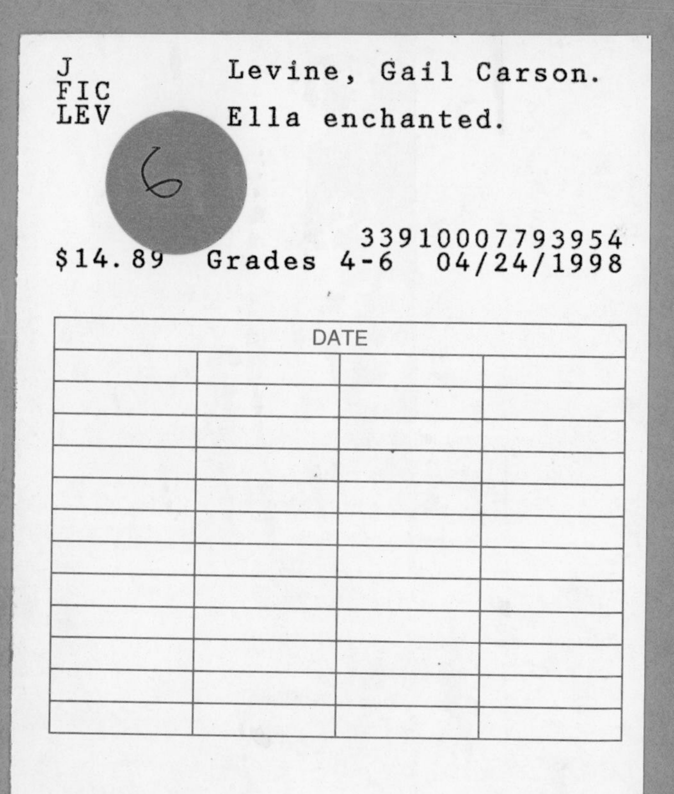

Levine, Gail Carson.

Ella enchanted.

6

33910007793954

$14.89 Grades 4-6 04/24/1998

DATE			